REQUIEM

ALSO BY T. G. AYER

Young Adult Paranormal

THE VALKYRIE SERIES

Dead Radiance

Dead Radiance Audio

Dead Embers

Dead Embers Audio

Dead Chaos

Dead Chaos Audio

Dead Wrath

Dead Silence

Joshua - Dead Radiance

Joshua II - Dead Embers

Joshua III - Dead Chaos

Joshua IV - Dead Wrath

Joshua V - Dead Silence

THE HAND OF KALI SERIES

Fire & Shadow

Blood & Gold

Time & Fate

Fury & Virtue

Spirit & Soul

∾

THE DARKWORLD ORIGINS

Pyros (Logan)
Ailuros (Kailin)

~

THE DARK SIGHT SERIES

Dark Sight
Cursed Sight
Vissarion
Shadow Sight
Dark Prophecy
Cursed Prophecy
Shadow Prophecy

~

THE APSARA CHRONICLES

Immortal Bound
Gods Ascendent
Dominion Falling
Vengeance Born
Last Legion

~

A SEASON OF ASH AND BONE

Heartfyre

~

Adult Sci-Fi

HANDS ASSASSIN

Death Dealer
Death Mark
Death Strike
Hand's Assassins Series

∾

NEW ADULT CONTEMPORARY THRILLER W/A TONI VALLAN

Beautiful Collision
Beautiful Conviction

∾

PSYCHOLOGICAL HORROR W/A TONI VALLAN

Dark Shadows
Splinter

REQUIEM

THE IRIN CHRONICLES BOOK 2

Copyright © 2014 by T.G. Ayer

All rights reserved.

Cover art by Eduardo Priego

Cover art © T.G. Ayer. All rights reserved.

ISBN-10: 0995112592

ISBN-13: 978-0995112599

REQUIEM

USA TODAY BESTSELLING AUTHOR

T.G. AYER

AUTHOR'S NOTE

The DarkWorld Universe, currently the SkinWalker Series and the SoulTracker series also includes the Irin Chronicles. The Irin Brotherhood act under a veil of secrecy, and have done so for centuries. The various councils within the DarkWorld are aware of the existence of the Irin operatives but the regular guy on the street has no clue.

So Kailin and Logan, Melisande and Saleem, and the rest of the characters from the DarkWorld—who you have probably already met—are going about their merry way with no clue that Evie and her team are also working to keep the world safe.

As yet, their paths have not crossed, but they do later in the series.

If you haven't picked up the SkinWalker or SoulTracker books yet, you may want to start with Skin Deep to get a feel for the Universe.

Alternatively, you could read Irin 1 & 2 and then run through the other DarkWorld books bearing in mind that both the Skin-Walker and the SoulTracker series have active crossover scenes.

There will be more to come in the DarkWorld Universe—DeathTalker and the Iron Queen likely to be one of the first to be released in the next year, telling the characters' stories from their own points of view, and shining a light on who they are and what their own lives look like.

T.G. Ayer
    The DarkWorld

CHAPTER 1

TWO WEEKS TO THE ASCENSION
CEREMONY

*E*vie stared at her hands and wondered, not for the first time, why they didn't shine with the blood she'd spilled a few days ago. She flexed her fingers, turning her hands over to study them in the light of the blazing fire. Long lean fingers, neatly manicured nails. Elegant hands for a cold-blooded killer. Only the slightly darker calluses on the inside of her fingers hinted at the hours of weapons-practice, hours of using weapons to kill.

She was used to being the executioner, although never guilty of ending an undeserving life. Not until the insidiously evil Marcellus Bactor had taken over as the Master of the Brotherhood of the Irin. As a warrior under the Brotherhood she'd performed missions of charity, missions of freedom, and of course missions of death. But under Marcellus death had become the sole function of the Irin.

Breakfast had not appealed to her at all. She hadn't expected to feel so strange after dispatching Marcellus. He'd been running the Brotherhood, his own needs more important than those of the humans whom they were all meant to protect. And, now she knew he'd killed her guardian, Patrick, and robbed her of the only father she'd ever known.

And yet here she was, feeling as though she ought to receive some sort of punishment for murdering the Master of the Irin. And for the first time she wondered what the Brotherhood and all her fellow Nephilim were doing right now. Choosing another Master? Perhaps Daniel? She shuddered at the thought. What was that saying? Frying pan and fire.

She sighed and shifted in the sofa, moving her cheek away from the warm flames of the fire. Julian's study was warm and cozy, and modern. Unlike anything she'd ever expected to see deep within the bowels of the earth. Dark wood shelves covered the walls filled to overflowing with books from every age, in every language. Comfortable sofas in earthy tones were scattered around the space, convenient spots for curling up with an interesting read. She tossed her dark hair over her shoulder and away from the heat from the fireplace.

She smiled at the memory of Castor's reaction to Marcellus' death just hours ago. He'd barely blinked on seeing the bloody remains of their old Master. Not that she should have expected tears considering Castor had borne the brunt of Marcellus's fury when Evie had left Greylock Estate in search of the Underworld. Evie's stomach tightened when she thought of Castor's little home on the grounds of the estate. A place the half demon had loved, a place now burnt to ash. But Castor's woes didn't seem to worry him too much right now. He was being well entertained by Pollo and his eclectic band of servants.

Julian had gone off on an errand in a bit of a hurry; something about a volcanic eruption in the South Pacific. That left Evie to her own devices, which wouldn't have been so bad if she had not needed to worry about Persephone. Evie was constantly on guard where the cold-hearted goddess was concerned, what with Persephone having already tried once to kill her. But so far she didn't seem to want to repeat the attempt. Maybe she was concerned about what Julian would do to her should she succeed. Evie snorted. No chance she'd let her guard down though.

Evie's skin tingled and she glanced at the shifting letters tattooed into her skin. They seemed alive, twisting and writhing beneath the surface of her pale skin like living things. Something Evie was yet to get accustomed to. She studied the markings then returned her attention to the pages of the ancient book lying open on her lap.

A book of dead languages, scripts from a time long gone. Perhaps a source of information, perhaps a way to undo this curse that she'd brought upon herself. Twelve seals to make a god. Not a bad way to turn an angel into the King of the Underworld.

She suppressed another sigh and rubbed her forehead. Suddenly the room seemed to close in on her and she felt desperate to leave the confining comfort of the study. She'd been on edge for hours now. What she probably needed was a sparring session. Something she wasn't likely to get down here.

She shut the book and left it on the sofa, heading for the door on feet that seemed to think she was in a hurry to be somewhere. Outside, the cool air from the shadowed tunnels teased her overly warm cheeks. She glanced up and down the passage listening for the sounds of approaching feet or hooves. Nothing. Torches shone at both ends of the tunnel, their flickering yellow light dancing and reflecting against the ominous jagged black stone of the tunnel walls.

Evie let her feet guide her, although part of her knew exactly where they were leading her.

CHAPTER 2

Uneven black stone gave way to a carved lintel, the three sides engraved with glowing letters in a language similar to those that marked Evie's forearm. Blue flames flared at her feet as she paused in the doorway, flickering at her. She didn't fear them now, knowing she could walk through them at will. Yet she waited because they seemed to be a way for the angel to retain a little privacy, what with not even having a door to his cell.

She herself could not keep away. She was drawn to him, had to speak to Gavriel again despite his own reluctance to talk. Gabriel. Gavriel. The names were so close. Had Patrick made a mistake. Could the two possible be that same person?

A thousand questions contorted Evie's dreaming and waking thoughts and not even her post-murder mood had affected her need to see the angel again.

She watched him now. He knelt in the center of the circular cell, his hands hidden in his lap. He had his back to her, the muscles taut and wiry, revealing the strength he tried to hide. Tears pricked her eyes. The wounds were still red and gory. And white where splintered bone stuck out like icy thorns. Only a few hours had passed but already there were visible signs of healing. Congealed blood crusted the edges of the wounds surrounding the shattered bones where magnificent wings had once joined with his body. The tightening of his neck, the slight tilt of his head told her Gavriel knew she was there.

"Come inside, Evangeline." His voice was raspy, husky, as if he barely used it. "Walk right through. The fire is an illusion," he said and she could almost picture a smile on his face.

Evie stepped through the line of twisting fire, making it past the flames, still very impressed by the illusion.

"So what's the point of having it there if it isn't real?"

Gavriel turned to Evie, giving his bare shoulder a tiny shrug. She almost cringed thinking any movement of his shoulder must hurt like hell. "It keeps away the curious. Some of the inhabitants of Hades realm think I am an oddity." His mouth curved in a self-deprecating smile.

Evie bristled. "You're not a freak show," she said, biting the words out with tamped down fury. She was incensed at the thought that anybody would come here just to get a look at the tortured angel, as if he were in a circus or a zoo, to be stared at and pointed at. She shuddered at the thought.

"I am an angel, cast forth from the bosoms of Heaven, now suitably incarcerated in the realms of the Underworld where I belong," Gavriel said, scorn dripped from the words as he uttered them. His gaunt features seemed more sunken than the last time she'd seen him, his cheekbones two stark points on his face. Remarkable how good he looked for an unkempt prisoner. "Who would not be curious?" he asked, with a small tilt of an eyebrow. It galled her to think that he accepted the idea of such an audience.

Evie felt a stab of guilt. Wasn't she herself one of the gawkers he was referring to? Hadn't she been unable to control the unspoken need to keep coming back to see him? Was she just like the mindless masses here to see the freak?

"But you are different, are you not?" Gavriel's voice broke through her thoughts, as if he could hear her inner conflict.

"What do you mean?" she asked, glancing at the angel's shadowed features. The torches on the walls around them jittered on an unseen breeze and Evie wondered why they hadn't provided Gavriel with a little warmth at least. A fire maybe? Or clothing more suited to the temperature of the stone cell. Wasn't hell supposed to be all fire and flame anyway?

Gavriel's voice drew her attention back. "Until recently, I had assumed I was the only angel in this hellish place." He stared at her face, his pale grey eyes gleaming in the torchlight.

"You know?" The words came out in a soft whisper. She looked away, unable to hold his penetrating gaze. When she met his eyes again she saw no judgment. Not that it made her feel any better. "How?" she asked, curious how he'd found out about her true nature. Not even Julian knew what she really was and she wasn't looking forward to breaking the news to him.

Gavriel smiled, the expression almost fatherly. And a little indulgent. "Angels have a sense of smell that goes deeper than just the scent of the body. We can smell those just like us. And those not so much like us." He paused and gave Evie a smile. "And angels have the power to see through all glamor."

A chill slid through Evie and she stiffened. She'd thought her glamor protected her but she'd forgotten that angels had Sight. "I am not an angel. I am Nephilim." Evie lifted her chin as a rush on anger filtered through her. She felt slightly ashamed to admit her half-breed status to a full-blooded angel and she didn't like feeling that way. There wasn't anything about being Nephilim to be ashamed of. But though she knew it, she still felt the prickle of unease, the tiniest sense of being second rate.

Not good enough.

"Yes," said the angel, clearly unaware of her inner war. "That explains the strength of your scent and why I took that much longer to figure out what you were. What are you doing here?"

He scanned her face as he posed the question. She returned his keen gaze accepting that lying to him was not an option.

"It was an accident." She gripped her hands before her, twisting her fingers together.

"And accident? What kind of accident results in an angel falling to hell?"

"An Alice in Wonderland type of accident?" she offered with a smile only moments before realizing he might not understand what she meant.

But he responded with a smile. "I see. So you fell through a hole in the ground, and ended up in Hades."

"Something like that." Evie smiled at the analogy. The only difference was she had come willingly with both eyes open.

"And why are you still here?"

"Because Alice is stuck here until she can turn back into herself."

He regarded her, a quizzical smile plastered across his face.

"So how much time do you have left?"

"A couple of weeks. What about you? How long are you supposed to stay here for?" Evie was desperate to change the subject.

"Oh, let's see... eight centuries and ... well... forever." His expression was serious and Evie didn't like it one bit.

"Forever?" She frowned, finding herself slightly annoyed with him. She wouldn't appreciate it if he was being facetious, but his expression remained serious. "I still don't think the time fits the crime."

"Oh, it fits. The law is the law. And I broke the law." A strange sadness tinged his words and he looked off into the distance, perhaps all the way to the past.

"What law was that?" Evie snapped. "Just because you serve Heaven does that mean you are banned from loving? I thought love was the whole point to Heaven's purpose?"

The angel raised his hand. "You don't understand ..."

His expression was so sad Evie felt the physical pain of it course through her heart. "Then make me understand. Tell me." Evie's muscles stiffened with anger as she stared Gavriel down, waiting for an answer. How could he be accepting of such a punishment, despite being in such pain because of it?

The angel sighed, his shoulder bowing forward slightly. "I made the greatest mistake - to fall in love with a Human. Worse yet - our union produced a child." Evie heart lurched. Her own mother had been human, had died in childbirth as all human women do when birthing an angel's child.

"She died." Evie's whispered words echoed around the angels cell, reflecting back on her the sad inevitability of a human woman's life should she chose to love an angel.

"No." He got to his feet and shook his head, a smile curving his lips. In that smile she saw a little of the happiness given him by the woman he'd loved. "It happens sometimes. The woman survives. She was weak after the birth, but alive. We went away, thought we could hide our little family. But they found us. They came for us. They killed her and took the child. And I fled. I searched for her. All over the world. But I never did find her. I searched until I was captured and brought here." His words came out short and hesitant, as if telling the story hurt him deeply, as if just speaking it out loud ripped open the old scars of loss and pain. During their conversation, Gavriel had kept moving around, his chains clinking as he shuffling along on dirty bare feet.

But Evie was no stranger to loss and pain. "I think I can understand some of that. My father left me with a friend. My guardian was good to me, told me much about my own father and his deeds. He didn't know my mother though. I've searched too. But my father seems to have disappeared. I'm so afraid he's dead and I may never know who my mother was. Or what kind of a person she was." Evie was unable to hold back the raw pain in her voice. But strangely enough it didn't embarrass her to reveal this part of her heart to Gavriel. He was the only person around that could understand what she felt.

The angel lifted a rickety broom from the ground and busied himself, sweeping up most of the feathers which littered the floor, gathering them into a small metal dustpan. Gavriel glanced up at Evie, his hooded eyes seemed darker as he spoke, "What is his name? I may have an idea of where he might be, provided I know his name."

Gavriel was busy tipping a dustpan filled with feathers into a black bag. Evie hesitated only a moment before answering. "Gabriel. That's the only name I have." At Evie's words, he froze, the muscles in his back stiffening, the cords in his neck tight. The angel turned to Evie as she spoke her father's name.

"What did you say?" He hesitated as he met Evie's eyes then tried to downplay his surprise by concentrating on sweeping up a far corner of the cell.

Evie repeated the name a little louder and kept a solid eye on the angel's expression. The muscles in his face remained relaxed, giving away nothing. He hid his emotion well, but not well enough for Evie to miss the expression that flickered in his eyes.

"Who is he? Your foster father ... what is his name?" His cleaning task all but forgotten, Gavriel stared at Evie, his voice filled with a desperation unlike any she'd heard before.

"Patrick Duarte. He was an Immortal."

"The Grand Master of the Irin. Yes, I remember Patrick. He is good man. You are lucky to have him as a guardian."

"Was," Evie said flatly the loss of Patrick still easily striking her to the core.

"Was what?"

"Patrick *was* a good man. He's dead." The words fell from her lips, each one weighed deeply with her loss. Evie felt tears fill her eyes as memories of her good friend and mentor visited her.

"Patrick is dead?" The angel whispered, the pain in his voice clear to Evie. So he'd known Patrick well enough to care that he'd died. She watched as Gavriel frowned, then asked, "How?"

Evie blinked back her tears. "Marcellus Bactor is how. He was the new master of the Irin. He ousted Patrick in what seemed like a 'peaceful' coupe," Evie said, forming quotation marks with her fingers when she said the word *peaceful*. "I'd suspected he had something to do with Patrick's death, but nobody believed me. Just before I discovered Patrick's body I overheard Marcellus tell his assistant that the deed was done. Only later did I realize the deed was murder." The single word echoed around the cell like an accusation. "Now, with Patrick dead, I'm totally alone. I'm more sure than ever that I want to find my parents. I need to know who they were as people..." Evie trailed off into silence.

Gavriel sighed. "What did Patrick tell you about your father?"

Evie twisted her fingers again. "That he was an angel who had fallen when Lucifer made his stand. That he longed to go back home, and had to adapt to living on Earth because of that longing. That he dedicated himself to eradicating the evil spawn of angels and humans, as part of his penance. And that he fell victim to the same emotion he despised in other angels. Patrick told me my father brought me to him because he was certain that my life was in danger. That was the last he heard of him."

When Evie looked up she saw the angel's expression and her stomach twisted. She recognized pain and grief on Gavriel's face.

"Did you know my father? He was also an angel. You may have known him." Evie looked at him hopefully, her gaze urging him to tell her something, anything she could hold on to.

But Gavriel just shook his head and said nothing, his eyes now devoid of any emotion. Maybe the armies of angels were too numerous for everyone to know each other, Evie thought. Or maybe Gavriel had other reasons for not admitting he knew her father.

She straightened, throwing her shoulders back despite the weight of her glamored wings. It didn't matter that he refused to help her. It didn't change her purpose. "I will find him. Even if I have to search my whole life, I will find him." She clenched her jaw, tamping down the strangest need to burst into tears. She'd always considered herself strong, stronger than most, if not all, her fellow Nephilim in the brotherhood. But now she felt helpless, nothing more than a lost child.

"That is a whole lot of years to spend searching. What if he does not want to be found?" he asked, challenging her with his pale eyes.

"That's preposterous. Why would he not want his daughter to find him?" Evie was incensed at the thought. More than that she was furious with Gavriel for even suggesting such a thing.

But he seemed oblivious to her fury as he shrugged a bare shoulder and said, "Things happen, sometimes people want different things. Have you thought about what you would do if you did find him and he wanted nothing to do with you? You need to be prepared for all possible scenarios."

Evie shook her head, every cell in her body denying the possibility that he'd just voiced. But even as she denied it she recognized the truth he spoke. She didn't have to like it but he was right, although the thought that her own parents would not want her was too hard to accept, especially now that she was feeling exceptionally lonely in the wake of Patrick's death.

She stared at Gavriel but there wasn't even a hint of apology in his eyes. She tried to cover the hurt she felt with a small smile.

"I know it is difficult to accept but you must be prepared for anything. Those who search may not always find exactly what they are looking for."

Evie nodded then mumbled an excuse about having to see Julian before she hurried out of the icy cell.

Hurrying away from the one place that had drawn her so many times. She didn't think she'd want to visit with Gavriel again any time soon.

CHAPTER 3

*E*vie made her way back to Julian's study, suddenly looking forward to sitting in front of the fire, looking forward to forgetting everything for a while. Gavriel's words had sown a frigid seed in her heart, for the first time making her feel unsettled about her relentless search for her parents.

She pushed the door open and smiled when she saw Julian pouring himself a drink, standing beside a cart laden with the lunch spread. "Hey. You're back." When the words left her mouth she blushed and felt a little stupid.

Talk about stating the obvious.

Julian returned her smile. Leaving his drink on the bar he walked slowly toward her. They stopped within inches of each other, Julian's eyes staring at Evie's face, as if he'd hungered just to see her. "How are you?" he asked softly his gaze flitting over her lips.

"Bored," she said with a grin. She felt awkward standing there in front of him. Until he rested his hand on her arm. The touch of his skin to hers set off a million tiny sparks, sending a shiver of anticipation up and down her spine.

She moved forward and so did Julian, until their lips were a hairs-breadth from meeting. Electricity sizzled between them and for a moment Evie's legs wobbled. She tipped forward toward him, reaching for Julian's shoulder to help steady her. Only touching his hard, muscled arm didn't help to steady her in any way.

Touching him set her body on fire, and she felt him shift, move toward her. He cupped the back of her head, tilting her face, giving him access to her lips.

And then he kissed her.

This time his exploration was not tentative. He kissed her hard, with a pent-up passion that felt dangerous and delicious all at the same time. Evie's heart thundered against her ribs as she kissed him back. She curled her arm around his neck and pulled him closer.

Julian's lips pulled away and Evie was about to protest when she felt him kiss her just below her ear. The warmth of his lips and the heat of his breath sent electric sparks surging through her limbs.

The door slammed open, the sound thrusting Julian and Evie apart. Pollo rushed into the study. In his excitement he'd thrown the door open without knocking. An oversight he didn't seem to notice.

"Trespassers, Your Highness." He took great big wheezing breaths and bent over, looking like he was about to fall flat on his face. He stuck his fingers into his side, poking at a stitch while trying to get his breathing under control.

"Trespassers? Pollo, Hades does not have trespassers. Everyone has a reason for being here," Julian said with a smile as he touched Evie's back tenderly, a silent apology for the intrusion. Evie hoped the rosiness of her cheeks was not obvious. Then Julian stepped away from her to face Pollo's agitation.

Pollo shook his head as if to shake off his fatigue. The fiery thatch of his hair fell away from the pair of dark brown filed-off horns that sat on either side of his head. The faun's excitement was infectious and Evie had to admit she was now dying to know who'd managed to enter the Underworld and get Pollo's knickers in such a knot.

"Very well, Pollo. Lead the way so that we can see these intruders for ourselves." Julian waved a hand at Pollo who blinked then nodded before spinning on one hoof and trotting out the door.

Julian followed the faun, giving Evie a conspiratorial smile over his shoulder. Evie stayed close to him, her footsteps adding to the urgent sound of hooves and shoes on the smoothed stone floor of the tunnels.

Up ahead, Pollo's ears twitched and he glanced over his shoulder at Evie. He threw her an odd look, one she wasn't sure how to define. Was he irritated with her? Of course, technically she was the interloper. Was Pollo one of Persephone's sympathizers? She wasn't sure about that. He'd never shown the goddess more than the required respect. And besides, Sef had her own minions willing enough to do her dirty work. Perhaps Pollo was judging her for her friendship with Gavriel?

Evie's jaw tightened. She reminded herself that in the greater scheme of things the faun and his loyalties were the least of her concerns. Getting back topside was the most important thing to her. That and surviving the next two weeks.

They followed Pollo back through the warren of tunnels while Evie tried not to spend too much time studying a certain shapely rear end just in front of her. Tried and failed.

She hid a smile as the walked out into the central cavern where Cerberus had left Evie her first day in the Underworld. The same place she'd received the news from her half-demon half-human friend Caster that led to the death of Marcellus, Master of the Irin.

Evie stiffened at the sight. Huddled and chained together in the center of the cavern sat two girls, surrounded by a quartet of guards whose spears were aimed directly at the pair. A little spurt of joy trilled through her, followed suitably quickly by a wave of worry. Both black haired and fiery eyes, the girls glared at their captors, their eyes promising vengeance as soon as their bonds were untied.

None of the guards knew the power they faced as they pointed their weapons at two very powerful, and now very angry, Nephilim. Evie was both shocked and overjoyed to set eyes on them though.

"Evie. Oh my, Evie. We thought you were dead." Ling struggled ferociously against her bindings only pausing when the sharp end of a spear was pointed perilously close to her eye by an over-enthusiastic faun guard. Way too close for Ling's comfort. And Evie's. A burst of irritation at the guards rippled through Evie. She was beginning to lose patience with the bumbling idiots.

Ling threw Evie a questioning look, waggling her eyebrows at the pointy bit hovering near her cheek. Ash on the other hand, sat still and stiff beside the struggling Ling. Uh-oh. Evie knew the guards wouldn't have much chance if she didn't prevent Ash from taking her fury out on them for her imprisonment, however short it was.

Ash stared down the fauns, her nostrils flaring as if they hadn't bathed in days and she found the odor revolting. Bound as they both were they'd been unable to shuck out their wings to escape the faun's clutches. A good thing as far as Evie was concerned. She rushed to their side. And when the spears were turned onto her in unison, she brushed them aside just as she heard Julian bark his orders to the guards to hold off.

Julian moved forward as Evie made quick work of the rope, releasing both girls within seconds. She helped them to their feet to a chorus of groans and massaged butts and knees. Hugs were exchanged before the two harassed Nephilim turned dangerous glares at their former captors.

Evie smiled and ignored the tension simmering between

Nephilim and slightly embarrassed guards. "Julian, these are my friends, Ling Han, and Ashika Deva." Although the girls bowed their heads, neither offered their hands to Julian. That may have been construed as bad manners had they not so recently been abused at the hands of his own guards.

He smiled at them, not in the least bit offended. "I see Evie's friends are as industrious as she is."

"We try," Ash said dryly, giving Evie the my-what-a-hunk look behind his back. Ling's lips just turned up in a silly, infatuated smile that brought an answering grin to Evie's lips.

A burst of joy filled her now that they were both here. The last thing she'd have thought possible was to have company while stuck in Hades. And at last she could share some of her fear and worry with her closest friends.

Julian cleared his throat and said, "Come, you must have some refreshments. I fear our hospitality leaves a lot to be desired." He threw a furious glare at Pollo and his guards who all had the grace to stare at the ground. "Pollo, follow me. I'll deal with you once the ladies are safely in my rooms."

Julian walked ahead and Evie followed with her two friends bringing up the rear. They said nothing as they traveled through the tunnels and Evie was aware that this would be a new experience for the girls.

At last they reached the study and Julian shoved the door open and waved them inside. "Pollo, I trust you will ensure that sufficient refreshments will be provided for our visitors. Immediately." Julian's tone was clipped and cool as he stared at the faun, whose face remained implacable now.

Julian left the room with Pollo in tow and Evie suspected the faun would be getting a solid telling off very soon.

Ling sighed and snuggled into the cushions at her back. Ash cleared her throat. "So, *that* is the reason we haven't heard from you in two months?" Her tone dripped ice but the look in her friend's eyes told Evie that Ash had missed her. And been worried.

"Two months? But I've been a little over two weeks," Evie protested, but even as she spoke she knew the Ash was right. Time moved slower down here in the underworld. Evie clenched her hands, curling them into fists. She'd wasted so much time.

"Nuh-uh. It's been two whole months. And we couldn't take it anymore. Marcellus was getting out of hand and then he up and disappeared a few days ago. We had no idea if he'd found you and killed you."

Though tempted to tell the girls of Marcellus' happy demise she wanted more information out of them first. "How did you guys know where to find me?"

"Did you see Castor yet?" Evie understood.

"You followed Castor? He will be hurt if he thinks you didn't trust him," said Evie wondering where the half-demon had gotten to. She made a note to send him a message so he could meet the girls.

"Trust is not an issue," Ling said shaking her head. "Marcellus' fury was something to behold. He focused on Castor for some reason and shocked the entire Brotherhood when he burned the poor guy's hut down. Castor was acting a bit strangely, and mentioned something about Marcellus coming for you. So Ash and I kept an eye out on him because we knew you'd want us to. Then we saw him run off to meet a certain albino demon. A little bit of prodding later we had the location to the entrance to this underground resort." She waved a hand airily around her head.

"I hope you left him in one piece," I said, grinning.

Ash snorted. "Don't worry, he still has all his parts. And for the record I do have eyes. That's a pretty hot demon if you don't count the albino part. And the demon part."

"That's good. I kinda need him in possession of all his parts. Or else I risk losing his cooperation."

"My pleasure. Although you should be happy we didn't have

the old kill first ask questions later rule," said Ash as she studied her manicure.

Ling snorted. "More importantly, we've found you. We knew it wouldn't be long before Marcellus got to you too. That imp is too unpredictable for my liking. We needed to do something. I couldn't stand sitting around on my butt anymore."

"So... new rules? What about your missions?"

"What missions? Once Marcellus found the Seals gone he ceased the seek and destroy missions and all we've been doing is school and nothing." Ling twisted her lips in distaste. "We aren't even allowed to leave the compound.

"Not even the Humanitarian missions?" I asked hopefully.

"Discontinued. Don't look at me like that. You have no idea what that pygmy has put us through. He knew he couldn't touch us, but we've been moved out of our rooms into dormitories in the old wing."

Evie had to choke on her laughter. Marcellus, the pygmy? Too funny.

"Co-ed dorms too." Ash wrinkled her nose in disgust. "Not that there is even a decent guy to be found. Just Flash but he has the hots for anything that smiles at him."

"And you are in danger," Ling said.

"Marcellus decided to pin the whole thing on you. He told the council that you blamed him for Patrick's death and wanted revenge. That's why you apparently stole his treasures and left Greylock. He vowed to follow you."

"The council ... did they believe him?" I asked, curious as to where the Brotherhood's loyalties lay. How strong was their faith in their rabid new leader?

"Some do, some don't. So we thought it was best we find you. He's got his dogs looking for you and I think they may have tracked Castor here already."

"No. They didn't need to follow Castor. They would have already known I was here."

"How would they know where you were headed?" Ling asked, confused.

"Because of the Seals," Evie said, watching the girls' expressions.

Ling's eyes widened. "So you found out what the Seals were for?" she asked.

"Yeah, I found out," Evie said dryly as she slumped into the back of the sofa. She was still angry with herself for walking right into the mess she was now stuck in.

"What's that supposed to mean? We didn't come all this way to get one of your vague answers Eves." Ash sat up, glaring at Evie.

"Okay, calm down. I'll tell you." Evie pulled back her sleeve to reveal the angelic script engraved into her skin. The dark markings shimmered in the rooms cool light. At least they had the sense not to writhe around on her hand and freak the girls out. Both her friends stared at the engravings in dead silence.

"What the hell are those?" Ash breathed the question out raggedly.

"The Mark of Hades." Julian's voice rang out with Evie's intended words.

"What is the Mark of Hades?" Ling spoke the name emphasizing the words in an irreverently mocking tone.

Julian merely smiled at her tone. "It means you now address the Ruler of the Underworld."

Both girls stared at Evie as if she's just grown another head.

"What the hell is he talking about?" Ash whispered her eyes so dark that Evie began to worry. Glamor faded under extreme stress. And this pretty much counted as extreme stress.

"No need to whisper Ash, this is Julian. Or rather, this is Hades." Evie looked at Julian as she spoke, and he stared back as if daring her to tell her story. "Julian has been ruler of Hades for the last two thousand years."

The girls were silent, which didn't happen often. Ash was pale, and her wings began to shimmer in the air behind her. Ash, for all her projected badness, always reacted like this in times of serious stress. Now it meant Evie had to get them away from Julian immediately, if only to prevent him from seeing the Apsara's wings. Evie also had to ensure the girls both knew that no-one in the Underworld must know they were Nephilim.

She grabbed their arms and ushered them out of the room. "Sorry, Julian. They both look like they need to rest. I'll take them to my room."

Julian nodded although a frown marred his brow. "I understand. This must be a lot to process." Evie glanced over her shoulder as they left the room to see Julian staring at them, a strange look on his face.

She shuddered, hoping he hadn't seen Ash's glamored wings.

ONCE THE GIRLS were safely ensconced in Evie's rooms, she guided them to a set of sofas arranged beside her gigantic bed. She sat with them, until she was sure Ash had calmed down.

A few minutes later a knock sounded at the door and it swung open. Two fauns entered bearing trays of food and drink, which they lay on the low table in front of the sofas. Only when they left did the stiff silence dissipate.

"Food," said Ling.

"Is it safe?" asked Ash, ever the wary one.

"Of course it is. I'm still alive aren't I?"

The girls hesitated only a moment more before descending on the trays. Finger sandwiches, egg and mayo, tuna, ham, and a variety of small cakes and biscuits. And tea, coffee and juice. Pollo had thought of everything. She ought to thank him and decided she would as soon as she ceased being pissed off at him.

Their hunger sated, the girls turned their attention to Evie.

"What's the hot guy talking about you being the Ruler of the Underworld?" Ling asked sharply.

I looked at her and sighed, not bothering to remind her that Julian had a name. "Something happened when I brought the Seals to the Underworld. Before I got to Julian I ended up in a room with a huge stone table. Then the seals began to sing and spin around the table and all of a sudden I'm dragged onto the table with the symbols being seared into my skin. To cut a long story short there was some kind of transformation ritual and the Markings ended up engraved on my arm."

"But how can something like that just happen? Just because you were carrying the Seals shouldn't mean you get bloody job of the head honcho."

I snorted. "There is a safeguard. One final piece that acted as a key to the whole process. Julian was certain they had hidden the final piece to ensure the Seals could not accidentally be used to transfer the mantle. Just my luck I had the final piece with me."

"What?"

"You have the most amazing luck, don't you?" snapped Ash, finally pulling out of her subdued state.

"The piece was around my neck. Has been for hundreds of years. It was the medallion my father left for me." Evie pulled the thong out of the neck of her shirt and showed the girls the medallion. It was the most drab and unassuming piece, a dull metal circle inscribed with glyphs. Hard to understand it had been so vital to the transformation. "It closed the deal. Julian found me when it was over. I had almost passed out."

"So you were the key?" asked Ling in disbelief. "You're saying the next King of Hades would have needed that last piece to complete the transformation." When Evie nodded, Ling scoffed and shook her head. "So I take it the pygmy knew nothing about that?"

Evie shook her head. "The only problem now is that Julian is no longer Hades."

"What's the big deal about that?"

Evie sighed. "He is now mortal."

"This is just perfect." Ling managed to sound both angry and sad at the same time. Evie knew exactly how she felt.

"I have no idea how to get out of this apart from patiently biding my time until the Ascension Ceremony."

"Why would you want to?" asked Ash.

"Do you have any idea what I've been through and what's in store for me if I don't find a way out?"

Ash just glared at her with a raised eyebrow implying she was over-reacting.

Ling held up a hand. "Hey, calm down. At least we've found out who is really after the Seals..."

Evie raised her eyebrows and waited. "Who could it be besides Marcellus?" But even as Evie spoke she knew the answer.

"Daniel," said Ling. She sat back, a satisfied smile on her face.

Evie wasn't shocked. Daniel had been the most unlikely possibility. But on hearing his name her thoughts went right back to the night she'd been stuck in his office and overheard Marcellus confirm he had just killed Patrick. She'd found it odd then that the roles seemed to have been reversed but it had not struck her in any way besides being unusual.

"You know, that might not be so unbelievable. For a long time Daniel maintained the bumbling assistant facade, but when I overheard them speak the tone of voice he used with Marcellus was definitely one of authority." Evie nodded, turning the idea around and around in her head.

"And Daniel is after the Seals because he wants to be the next Hades?" asked Ash, her tone confirming she didn't think it so plausible.

"You are a smart cookie, you know that?" Ling remarked. Ash just mouthed 'Whatever' at her.

"That's why you guys raced here? To tell me about your suspicions concerning Daniel?"

"Yes, and about Marcellus." Ash replied as she got to her feet and inspected the room. She seemed to be drawn toward the tendrils of steam sneaking around the wall to the hot-pool.

Evie smiled. "Well, Marcellus is no longer a problem. He won't be bothering anyone anytime soon."

That got both girls attention. "What do you mean?" asked Ash. She spun around and stared at Evie. "What happened to him?"

"Let's just say he got his just desserts." Evie snickered.

"You're holding back." Ling tugged her arm, her eyes threatening Evie with dire consequences. As usual Ling loved drama.

"Okay, okay," Evie raised her hands in mock defense. "If you must know, he came down here to kill me and get the Seals but became Chimera chow instead."

"A Chimera ate him?" Ling's eyebrows greeted her hairline. "Eh, you mean he's dead?"

"You mean the Chimera is real?" asked Ash, her face a bit too pale to be healthy for a girl with her dusky complexion.

At Ash's question all three girls burst out laughing.

"Look, I'll have to tell you the whole story. Right now I have to speak to Julian about Daniel. He needs to know that someone is so dead set on getting the Seals that he is actually coming down to the Underworld. You girls get some rest."

CHAPTER 4

The news that Daniel was on the way to claim the Seals did not send Julian into a mad panic. Instead he sat down beside Evie and said, "We need to find a way to get you out of the hold of the spell." His forehead was marred by the ripples of a worried frown.

"I thought you said there wasn't a way to do that." Evie gave Julian her full attention, especially now that he was suggesting a possible way out from this fiasco.

"I have been thinking, especially since Sef's been so upset with you being the new Ruler." He rose and went to a glass-fronted bookshelf which he unlocked with a tiny gold key. He retrieved a book, so heavy he had to carry it in both his arms. When he sat he balanced the weight of it on his lap.

I snorted. "She's only upset because you're now mortal, and she can't legitimately get her claws into you since she is no longer your consort. With Hades out of the picture you were obviously her next choice." Evie knew she was taking a huge chance by voicing her opinions to Julian about Persephone. A few kisses didn't mean she had the right to challenge him on his relationship choices. They were close but not there yet. But she was curious about Julian's emotional attachment to Hade's scorned Queen.

"She will have a very long wait if that is her goal," said Julian without even glancing up from his tome. "There is no way, in this hell or others, that I would want to take Persephone as a consort. Or to have to face the music when Hades does finally return. I am here only on a temporary basis anyway."

Evie's stomach tightened at his words. He was saying he had no interest in the goddess and Evie hoped he spoke the truth. "I've been reading up as much as I can. There is almost nothing about this kind of spell or binding. Except this-" Julian turned the book toward her so she could read the ancient script. Evie looked at the mess of words and then back at Julian, wanting to laugh. The writing was ancient Greek or something close.

"Translation please?" She raised an eyebrow at him, softening it with a small smile.

"Oh. Sorry about that." He turned the book around and flipped a page, shifting close to Evie to study it. "I keep forgetting that not everyone else speaks eighteen languages."

"Showoff," Evie muttered.

"What?" Julian glanced up at her, the blank look in his eyes making it clear he was already deep within the words of the book.

"Oh, nothing," she responded. Turning her gaze to the page she pretended to be deep into the script too. He'd see right through that but she didn't care.

Julian continued, oblivious to her fake examination of the words. "What I have found is that the power of the mantle can be transferred to a willing recipient only if the giver- that will be you- and the receiver - a suitable other person- are in mutual understanding."

Silence fell upon Evie's ears and for a moment she couldn't believe what she was hearing. "Is this for real?" she breathed the question softly, as if afraid saying it out loud may destroy the fragile glimmer of a possibility of freedom.

"Yes, it says it right here." He nodded stabbing an elegantly sexy finger at the aged paper.

Evie's eyes went from word to finger to Julian's face. "But how can we be sure?" She knew she was hesitant, just in case reality was on its way to douse her with the truth. "Hades used this once on you and I'm only the second person to receive the mantle. How can we be sure it is safe?"

Julian shrugged. But from the look in his eyes Evie could tell he was worried too. "We can't. But trust this book; it is one of the Books of Fate. Many were said to be destroyed but I saved a few and brought them with me. There are mysteries explained in these books that make them extremely dangerous in the hands of the wrong person."

"Is that why so many of the books were destroyed?" The thought of the destruction of any book galled her.

"Yes. Humans are notorious for their greed. And their vanity."

"Like Marcellus and Daniel," said Evie scorn dripping from her words.

"Exactly. We both know where Marcellus is so that sorts one of your problems out."

"Yeah. That." Evie cringed at the memory of Marcellus's last screams before the Chimera had killed him.

Julian didn't seem in the least bit concerned that he sat beside a killer. "We just need to be in the right place at the right time when Daniel arrives."

"I'm still curious as to why Daniel desires the mantle." Evie frowned. "He's always seemed the underling, but it's clear now that he has another agenda."

Julian grunted. "The job of ruling the Underworld is all-encompassing. The myths about Hades made it look like it was a simple task encompassing stealing young maidens and tricking the sons of the Gods into remaining here forever. Most of those tales were just that, tales." He shook his head in disgust.

"So you didn't think about those issues when you started your ... role?"

Julian nodded, his eyes dark and serious as his memories traced his past. "Yes, I did. And that's what made it all the more shocking. Hades didn't have the time to be a playboy."

"So Sef may have been disappointed?" Evie felt slightly sorry for the goddess. Only very slightly.

"Disappointed?" Julian asked, his confusion evident in his twisted brow.

"Yeah. Carried off, swooning in the arms of a gorgeous hunk of a God only to become a trophy wife to a Ruler who had other things on his mind." Evie shook her head and clicked her tongue in mock sympathy.

"I think you may be more right than you realize," Julian mused. "This job is terribly responsible. Hades controls, or rather, tries to achieve a balance to Earthly disasters. Volcanoes, earthquakes, plate movements, geothermal activity, seabed earthquakes, landslides, the list goes on."

"So, anything to do with the underground is your deal?" asked Evie.

"Yes. Even when its under the sea. Poseidon doesn't like it when I use his waters to inspect seabed activity, but it can't be avoided. He just has to accept my trespass when it is needed. I guess you could say that he puts up with me."

"You sound like you know a lot about geology."

Yeah, another dumber question, Evie.

But she had to admit she was fascinated now that Julian had revealed exactly what he'd been up to whenever he'd run off on his sudden errands.

He nodded. "I had to learn. I didn't want to be like Hades and think that everything that happened underground was because some God sneezed or burped." Julian looked disgusted.

Evie laughed and stared at him, finding it hard to believe. "Did Hades really think that?"

"Yes. And so did many Gods and people at that time. Everything changed with science and even Gods had to relearn how the Earth really worked. Its a lot like living on a live creature. We have to learn how the planet works to adapt to its changes."

Evie was impressed at Julian's description of the interaction of gods and the planet Earth. An interesting way to put it and one that made immense sense. "Guess you'll be in charge of mining materials won't you?" she asked.

"You are smart." Julian nodded in approval. "All solid and liquid mined materials from diamonds to oil - that's my territory. I do my best to ensure Humans miss the deposits as much as possible. No use in letting them take everything now. Before long there will be nothing left for the future generations. And people are yet to learn the true value of diamonds and oil."

For a moment Evie was silent as she wrapped her head around Julian's role. "So it is possible that Daniel has a bigger plan than we thought. Do you think he is making a play for control of gold or oil?"

"Quite possible. Even probable."

"But how would he have found out about the real role of Hades when the myths have done such an excellent job of hiding it?"

"It's not a secret. You just have to be smart and industrious and reach the right conclusions. If you know what you are looking for you are bound to find some of the truth if not all of it. Even the old philosophers and poets told the truth in many of their works. Although they often glamorized it or downplayed it, depending on their moods of course."

"Or their political leanings?" Evie suggested.

"Yes. That too. So our only solution is the transfer of the mantle."

"Who will be willing to take that responsibility? Surely not

Persephone?" Evie fairly gagged at the thought. The shrewish female as the Ruler of the Underworld? Not a very palatable thought.

"I know someone suitable for the job. Someone with previous experience."

"Er, there are only two people with previous experience and one of them hasn't found himself yet. The other, I think, is officially crazy to think I would agree." She sat back and folded her arms, staring straight ahead, her body stiff.

"Come now, Evangeline. This is the most sensible option." Julian leaned forward and pulled her around to face him.

She looked at him reluctantly, her arms tensed. "What's so sensible about it?" she demanded. "It would mean banishing you to the Underworld again for heaven knows how many more millennia." Evie shook her head, not liking the idea at all. "Probably the only good thing would come of it is you would get you immortality back." Hearing those words made Evie feel like what Julian was suggesting may be worth it. Still, it made him Hades again, stuck down here in the Netherworld. She had to admit she was being selfish; how did one have a relationship with the God of the Underworld while maintain ones own life? Maybe that just wasn't an option.

Julian tilted his head and grinned. "I'd also get Persephone back too." Evie had to smile back at him. At least he had a sense of humor. But she couldn't find anything amusing about the prospect of exiling Julian again.

"But you lost so much when Hades took you."

"I gained so much too," he replied. "Tell me, where will you be in a thousand years?"

Evie didn't answer.

"If I were mortal I would have been dead for more than nine hundred of those years, Evangeline. If I were immortal I'd still be here." It was a sobering thought. All Evie had been thinking about was the unfairness of the young Julian being taken from the only family he had ever known. He'd missed his chance to take back a throne that had belonged to him, missed the chance of a reunion with his mother Julia.

Evie had been so absorbed in the hurt of his past, she had not thought about his future. A future for him as a newly changed mortal meant he would have to die a slow death in a world so alien from his own. And she would have willingly given him that choice. But she wasn't ready to admit she was being convinced.

Julian closed the book and returned it to the glassed-in shelf. Then he came to stand in front of her, holding out both his hands he waited for her to take them. "Let's go for a walk. I have something I think you would like to see." When she placed her hands in his he lifted her to her feet and ushered her toward the door.

CHAPTER 5

*J*ulian walked through the warren of tunnels with Evie at his side. Their silence was companionable. Evie, meanwhile, had her thoughts fairly divided between Gavriel's agonies in body and Julian's agonies in mind.

They'd traveled through the dark passageways until the stone ground gave way to softly packed sand that made Evie think of the seaside. Up ahead the tunnel grew gradually brighter and Evie recognized sunlight, bright beams alternating wide and thin, streaming its warmth into the rocky passage. The tunnel led upwards to surface in the middle of a valley.

When she glanced around, Evie did a double take. The valley was nature's most beauteous bounty, beautiful and filled with life.

Julian led the way, taking hold of Evie's hand. He curled his fingers between hers and walked at a slow pace, allowing her to enjoy the sights she passed in such awe.

Trees bearing fruit she'd never seen before, their leaves unusually shaped, their trunks covered in barks of a hundreds of different earthy shades. Evie saw plants and flowers few humans would have touched or smelled. She felt so blessed that hot tears singed her eyes. This sight was so far from the dead and barren valley she'd seen on entering the Underworld. It was like a totally different world altogether.

"What is this place?" she whispered.

"The Garden of Ep. The place of the pure souls. After judgment, every soul seen to be of pure goodness comes to this field. This is where they spend the rest of their lives.

"My kind of Hell, I think," she said with a smile. A warmth bathed her cheeks and she looked up, expecting sunlight but there was of course none. The area above them glowed with a twisting swirling light from what looked like a far off galaxy. Orange and red and purple smoky brightness bathed the Orchard.

She glanced over at Julian who gave her an indulgent smile. "There are many of these havens all over the world. They are like small countries actually. And they exist for the same reason - to house the souls of the good."

"Thank you for showing me this." As entranced as Evie was she was also grateful for Julian's thoughtfulness. He'd showed her that banishment to Hades was not as bad as it looked. That for the good souls there was still the opportunity to enter a heavenly space to live out eternity.

"I wanted you to see that being the Ruler of the Underworld is not so bad a card to be dealt. If you want to keep the mantle I will understand but I owe it to you and to myself to show you the real Hades. Most people only know vaguely about the beauty we have here."

Evie nodded. "Thank you for showing me this place."

"I had hoped that it would help."

"It did." She smiled.

CHAPTER 6

*T*he next few hours were a tense amalgamation of minutes and seconds of fear and worry.

Julian had the whole place on high alert since Ling and Ash had brought the news of Daniel's intention to retrieve the Seals himself. Julian saw it as a threat to Evie's life, especially since she was the one who was bound by the Seals. But Evie considered Daniel a threat to Julian's life because of his lack of immortality and the role he'd played in the past two millennia. He may not be the current holder of the title, but it didn't make his power any less.

The problem was they had no idea when Daniel would decide to pitch up and stake his claim on the Seals. Julian was still insistent on his proposal to take the title again but Evie was yet to agree.

Evie walked into Julian's study to find a sullen Persephone, arms folded and face flaming, sitting opposite a darkly silent Julian. Her blond hair fell in ringlets around her face, hiding her expression although Evie knew it would not be pretty.

"Well, Evangeline, your timing is just impeccable isn't it?" The goddess lifted her eyes and glared icily at Evie.

"What did I do now?" Evie responded dryly. She was so tired of Sef's patronizing, cold manner. But there was no changing the iciness of the Bringer of Springtime. That was a bit of a joke in itself. It didn't seem logical that the goddess who was responsible for the season that brings life to the world was the same bitter, shrewish woman who'd been making Evie's life a perfect hell these past weeks.

"It is not what you are doing that is the problem. It is what you are not doing." Persephone clipped the words out, each one dropping like a sharp ice crystal.

"Which is?" Evie raised an eyebrow in question, the action and her question drawing twin spots of pink anger to Sef's cheekbones. Had it not been for the livid expression in her eyes she would have looked quite attractive.

"Leaving." Persephone rose to her full height, which though a good head shorter than Evie, was still impressive. Or would have been had the person she was confronting was one of her simpering slaves. Evie was not.

"As you well know, I can't leave, not until the Bonding has completed."

Julian shifted in his seat opposite the goddess. "Sef, I've already told you that this is not an easy decision to make. And it is not one you have any involvement in." Julian stared Persephone down, and although he used her affectionate name, his face held nothing to indicate he had a soft spot for her at all.

She watched his face for a moment and Evie wondered if she was hoping to see some expression on his face that would tell her that he cared about her opinion. Then her face hardened, her jaw clenching tightly. "Well, if you don't do anything about it, I certainly will." She lifted her chin defiantly.

"What do you propose to do then?" Julian asked, the vein at his temple throbbing. He too masked his fury and impatience with the goddess very well. Evie had to laugh at the civilized fury of the conversation.

"Escort the creature back to the gates," snapped Persephone before she turned her head abruptly to look away from him and directly at Evie.

"And what do you suppose that would get you?" Julian asked, his tone even, not once belying how laughable the goddesses plan was. Evie was getting annoyed with his patience.

"Rid us of her?" She threw Evie a dirty glance.

"Let me explain this to you, Persephone. The Binding is a spell that Hades cast over the seals." Julian spoke with the patience of a father to an especially unruly child. The mere mention of Hades name cast a grey pall over Persephone's face. If Evie didn't know the woman was a heartless viper, she would have thought the expression looked like longing. "The Binding holds the newly inducted ruler within the boundaries of Hades, in which time they are expected to learn what they can and decide if they wish to stay. I may not have received that luxury but Evangeline has. She will have to decide what she wishes to do. Remain as ruler, or leave."

"If she wasn't so selfish she would leave. Then you can take back the throne and your immortality too." The goddess cast Evie a glance that would have frozen Evie's blood in her veins had she been a frightened docile female. Good thing she was no such thing.

"It is not for you to decide," snapped Julian, at last giving in to the pent up frustration of the conversation. He took a deep breath before he continued. "And Evie has to wait out the full twenty-eight days of the Binding time."

Evie decided that silence would win her more points in this argument. Besides, there seemed to be something else that was bothering Persephone, something more than just vying for Julian's attention.

The Goddess of Spring knew when she had lost the battle. At Julian's words she got to her feet, turned and stalked out of the room in subdued fury. She had the air of an animal departing the fight, but not slinking away. She moved with purpose as if already planning her return. Evie didn't like it one bit and planned not to be around when Persephone regrouped for round two.

"How do you put up with her?" Evie asked as she stared at the empty doorway.

"You will be the one putting up with her soon enough." Evie's head turned sharply and she stared at Julian in realization that those words weighted the decision she needed to make.

"That means I'd be throwing you to that she-wolf again for another few thousand years," she said raising an eyebrow.

"Why does that worry you at all? Besides she is another man's wife. Older woman hold little interest for me." Julian smiled and closed the distance, drawing Evie to the sofa. "Evangeline, should you decide to exchange places with me I promise to try and find a way to make you immortal. That is what you have been worried about, is it not?"

His words made Evie aware that she had managed to keep her angelic identity a secret for so long. She wasn't sure how much longer she could get away with it, though. Not with Daniel's arrival looming. Evie also suspected that there were many people would be unhappy to see a child of Heaven running the black halls of Hell.

Slowly she realized she had made her decision. The spasm in the pit of her stomach had ended her doubt. The mere thought of seeing Julian die over the next few decades terrified her. At least if he regained his throne he would rule here. Perhaps she could return to visit.

"So, tell me, if I relinquish this right, could I still return to Hades?" She watched his face half afraid he would say she'd never be allowed to set foot in Hades again.

Julian smiled and Evie felt her tension ease. "Yes, absolutely. These markings on your arm-" Julian pushed back her sleeve and ran fingers of fire over her engraved skin. "They are the keys to the kingdom. You will no longer require the coins for Charon, nor will Cerberus need to be consoled to allow you to pass."

"And I can come back whenever I like?" Evie asked.

"Yes." Julian nodded and smiled, as if reassuring a child.

Evie looked down and studied the markings etched into the soft flesh of her arm, her own fingers tracing them, so close to Julian's, larger, sturdier digits. She'd been so concerned about the life he'd once lost so very long ago, had been so against throwing him back into servitude to Hades, that she'd completely forgotten that Julian may have his own opinion on the matter. It was clear from his argument that he had no qualms about taking the role on again. He'd sounded like he enjoyed the responsibility as well.

"Okay." She spoke softly, head still bent, staring at their hands just a breath apart.

"Mmh?" Julian bent his head closer. Evie nodded.

"Okay. I'll do it. But only if you want to. Only if you are sure." She searched his face, ready to withdraw her offer at the slightest hint of doubt.

"Good. I'm glad." He patted her hand again, this time holding on a tad bit longer than was entirely necessary. Which to Evie was entirely too nice for words. Heat rose in her cheeks and she hoped he didn't notice. "It's for the best. It will take me a while to find a way to make you immortal too."

Evie shook her head, almost spoke but no sound came from her throat.

Julian had no knowledge that she didn't need his immortality spells, and she didn't want him wasting his time finding one. The difficult thing was to avoid the topic of immortality. At least until she'd transferred the power back to him. Then she would be free to tell him exactly what she was.

"What?" Julian's face fell, disappointment clouding his eyes. "Don't you want me to find a way to make you immortal?"

"It's not that. There is something we need to talk ab-" Evie was saved by the sound of his hooves clip-clopping randomly first on hard stone and then, dully on the soft carpet as Pollo darted into the room.

"Intruder alert," Evie said softly.

They both faced Pollo who stood bent over, tufts of white hair quivering at his ears, in stark contrast to his rosy red cheeks.

"Where is he?" asked Julian as he bounded out of his seat. Evie's stomach did a somersault of fear.

Daniel.

"Cerberus." The faun wheezed out the word and pointed at the door. As if on command, an angry roar echoed through the tunnels. Goosebumps pebbled Evie's skin at the sound.

"Make sure that dog is unharmed. The last thing we need is for Cerberus to be hurt in the middle of all this mess."

Evie nodded in total agreement, feeling the same guarded affection for the three-headed pooch as Julian.

"Ready?" asked Julian.

"As I will ever be."

CHAPTER 7

*E*vie kept pace with Julian as they raced to the cavern, the sound of their pounding feet echoing louder as they approached the open space. Her sword clinked against her hip, an assuring reminder that whatever happened she would be able to defend herself and Julian. Evie suspected that Daniel was much more cunning than they'd given him credit for. He would very likely have found a way to get past Cerberus by now. And he'd be well on his way to reaching the Cavern.

Where they would soon meet him.

All the tunnels led to the centrally located Cavern which sat like a fat little spider with twelve skinny legs leading off it, spreading into the depths of the rock palace of Hades. It wasn't what she had imagined at all. Evie wasn't sure what she'd expected, though it was certainly not as grand as a Palace should be.

The Cavern was the Hall of Judgment, and it made sense that it was central to the structure of Hade's home.

Greek Mythology was Evie's worst subject and she was grateful to Patrick that she knew enough to get by. He'd always had a way of making things come alive. Evie recalled snippets of a conversation about the Underworld and Judgment.

She found herself delving far too deeply into faraway memories and pulled herself short.

For now her concentration should lie with the enemy. It was best to meet an enemy head on. And if there was ever a place so well suited to a fight it was the Cavern. Its high ceiling was at least fifteen feet off the ground, its sloped walls smooth and shiny. The bones of the original natural cavern had only been enhanced by the inhabitants of this world. The stone walls were carved in relief, scenes from Persephone's first arrival, and of Hade's meeting with Hercules. The frescoes brought with them the reality that Evie was very much out of her depth.

The entrances to each of the twelve tunnels were lit by a pair of burning torches. Errant waves of air rushed through the cavern and caused the torch-flames to flicker. Ghastly shadows danced beside the carved figures on the stone walls. Those breezes always un-nerved Evie as she was never very sure which tunnel provided the air and what mythical creature would follow the breeze. Cerberus and the Chimera were enough for anyone to deal with in the space of two weeks.

As they rushed into the Cavern, the flickering light fooled Evie's eyes into thinking the carvings were real. Her heart raced from both the headlong run to the Cavern and the eerie images which now surrounded them. Julian appeared unperturbed. Pollo's hooves clacked against the stone floor as he rushed in behind them. The faun's face gleamed bright red. That and his rapid breathing and it wasn't hard to guess he was frightened out of his wits. Evie had to assume threatening intruders were a rare occurrence in Hades. More often than not the threat of Hades itself would be a million times scarier than anything that would enter the underworld.

A rush of footsteps echoed from one of the tunnels snaking toward the Cavern; the one leading straight to Cerberus's lair.

Daniel would be unaware Evie had been fore-warned and his apparent lack of care to soften his footsteps confirmed his over-confident arrival.

Dark shadows spewed forth Daniel's gangly shape.

Daniel.

Daniel Feinstein, assistant to the Master of the Irin for almost a decade. He'd blended into the background, remained below the radar. Intentionally. Nobody had ever really known this man who had lived among them for a whole decade.

Now, the once mild-mannered, scholarly man stood before her, a passionate, feral gleam in his eyes.

Despite his rapid pace through the tunnels his breathing remained even and unaffected as if he'd merely taken a calm stroll along the beach. Evidently he was much stronger that his skinny frame implied. He stopped just inside the entrance and looked at Evie, giving Julian a transitory glance.

"Evangeline." He said her name, shaking his head as if she were an errant child caught in the middle of mischief. She remained silent, not at all sure what she was supposed to respond with.

"Daniel." She inclined her head determined to remain on a sure footing with him.

"I have come for the Seals, Evangeline." He spoke patiently, again as if convincing a wayward child. But his expression was unnerving, and Evie's heart tripped. A frightening darkness swam in his eyes, and Evie tasted fear in her throat. He muscles tightened, and power emanated from his body. Evie frowned and stared at Daniel. Something wasn't right. Fear rippled through her followed quickly by unease. Something inside her screamed at her but she couldn't understand what it was saying. Frustrated she clenched her fists then opened them, keeping her hand ready to reach for her sword. She was ready to fight him. He clenched his teeth then said, "I have waited far too long for this, you will not stand in my way any longer."

"Daniel, you are wasting your time here." Evie spoke, keeping her voice even, trying not to reflect the tumult of emotion within her. Not an easy task since she was slowly beginning to fear his fury. Something inside her sensed the depth of his anger. Knew she may have just taken on more than she could deal with. Even with Julian at her side, Evie guessed the winner may just be this once unassuming Grigori. "Marcellus has already tried, and failed to retrieve the Seals." She gained a deep sense of satisfaction to see the confusion in his expression.

"Where is Marcellus, now?" he asked, his hand also at the ready not a breath away from the hilt of his sword. "His men said when they'd left, he'd been with you?" Evie gritted her teeth. She refused to be guilty for Marcellus's death, and the last thing she wanted to do was doubt her actions just because Daniel expected it.

"What were you expecting me to do, Daniel? Provide him with five star entertainment?" Evie lifted her chin, but didn't miss Daniel's hesitation. She continued, "He got what was coming to him."

"What have you done with him?" Daniels voice vibrated on the question, the tremor in his voice indicating a deeper dark anger.

"Marcellus got what he deserved, Daniel. He had a lot to pay for. Including Patrick. You didn't think he would get away with it, did you? Sorry, but your Master is not coming back from where he is now." There was a certain satisfaction to those words that Evie enjoyed far too much. She tamped it down, ashamed.

"He was not my master." Daniel denied his servitude shaking with anger. "The only Master I have ever bowed to has forsaken me."

Evie scoffed. "So what are you going to tell me? That you were Marcellus's Master?" Daniel regarded her, his brow rising, impressed.

"You catch on fast for a half-breed." Evie glanced at him

sharply, surprised at the denigrating tone of the words. If he disliked Nephilim he'd certainly gotten the wrong job working among them for so many years. And if the roles of Master and servant were indeed in reverse to what the Brotherhood had understood, they'd kept that fact well under wraps. Memories of Daniel's constant presence when Marcellus was around flitted through Evie's mind. He'd never been far from Marcellus, that much was true. The pair had managed to pull the wool over everyone's eyes. The entire Brotherhood had believed a well-fashioned lie.

"Half-breed, not half-wit," spat Evie. "I see your true colors are finally showing, Daniel."

"You have no idea, little Nephilim." He laughed, the name of her kind rolling off his tongue like a vile profanity.

"Actually, we have a pretty good idea. We would have realized what you were up to soon enough." She lifted her chin, challenging him to deny it.

But he just shook his head. "And, naturally you would have been too late," Daniel sneered. "In fact, I think in your case you were too late for Patrick, weren't you?"

Evie's jaw tightened, her teeth jamming against each other. He was goading her and in spite of knowing that, every instinct screamed at her to race at him and claw his eyes out. But she didn't. She wouldn't allow her anger and grief to cloud her judgment. Daniel had proved to be smarter than them all. Now, she needed to be at the top of her game if she wanted to defeat him.

Evie circled Daniel. He smiled, not at all intimidated by her movement. He held his ground, turning his head to follow her movement. This was not his turf and yet he exuded a confidence which made Evie quake. There was something raw and powerful about Daniel. Something that warned Evie to back off. But she could not afford to listen to her instinct.

"Evie, stay away from him." Julian's voice rang out, tossed back and forth across the stone walls.

"Who is your guard dog, Evangeline?" asked Daniel, his lip curling in a nasty sneer.

"Julian is the guy in charge down here." Evie doubted that it mattered at all that Julian was the Ruler of the Underworld. To Daniel nothing mattered except for the Seals themselves. And, as if he'd heard her thoughts, Daniel spoke, "Why don't you just tell me where the Seals are and we can be done with all this nonsense."

"You aren't getting the seals Daniel. They belong to Hades, not you."

"So do you plan to stop me?" His fingers tightened around the handle of his sword.

"You know I can, Daniel."

"Evie, you are not seriously thinking of fighting this man are you?" Julian was shocked, and in that moment, looking at his narrowed eyes and flushed face, Evie realized there was one issue that could make this whole thing go straight down the tubes. During her time down here, she had kept the secret of her angelic nature from Julian.

In the beginning it had been a precaution in case her angelic nature would be a reason to be a target in the Underworld. And then it had been too late, too late to reveal her nature to Julian who had begun to trust her. Now it was too late to take those steps back to the beginning when she should have told him in the first place.

But hindsight was a wonderful tool for clarity. Not that it helped her now. All it did was mess with her mind and add to her fear and guilt.

CHAPTER 8

*E*vie's other hand hovered over her knife while her eyes remained fixed on Daniel's face. She didn't like the smirk that twisted his lips. Neither did she like the way Julian hovered in her line of vision. He wanted to protect her but this was certainly not the time. He was more of a distraction, what with his mortality posing a problem for both Julian and Evie.

Wounded, Julian was very likely to die, while Evie would live through anything Daniel could throw at her. He'd have to rip her to pieces to kill her. But Julian knew none of this. And the guilt twisted in her gut.

Daniel brandished a monstrous sword from his side and in that moment Julian stepped smoothly in front of Evie. The weapon gleamed an evil black and made Evie recall the vision she'd seen outside Gavriel's cell. For a moment she tasted blood and smelled it too. Just as it had smelled in the vision, pungent and visceral. There was something about the sword too that turned her gut and made her want to scream in agony.

Evie moved forward intending to get past Julian but he elbowed Evie out of the way. Daniel watched them, tossing the evil instrument back and forth between both hands. His skill with the weapon was clear to Evie; he handled the weapon as if it weighed as much as a toothpick but Evie knew it was brutally heavy. If it was really obsidian.

Evie's eyes settled on the bulge of muscles on his arms and shoulders, usually hidden beneath his unassuming Grigori cloak. Muscles that confirmed her opponent was strong and trained. Daniel had managed to keep a lot hidden these past years.

"Well, Ruler of Hades, show me what you got, then." Daniel lunged toward Julian who side-stepped him neatly and returned swiftly to his ready stance. He had no weapon. Pollo watched from the edge of the Cavern, prancing from one hoof to another his eyes flitting from his Master to the intruder and back again. The tap-tap of his hooves echoed eerily around the cavern, like a distant clock counting down Julian's last moments.

"A weapon for Julian, Pollo," Evie shouted at the frightened faun. Pollo's head shot up as her voice reverberated around the room, louder than it should be, louder than was natural for a normal girl. Stirred into action, Pollo raced off, his hooves clipping a serious pace down the nearest tunnel.

As Evie watched his tail disappear into the shadows of the tune she prayed he would return before Daniel ended his master's life.

Meanwhile, Daniel and Julian circled each other like a pair of bull elephants in must. She would not be surprised at all if they began stamping their feet and trumpeting.

"Julian, leave it. It's my fight not yours," Evie called out hoping he would listen.

"How do you expect to fight him? He could kill you," Julian yelled back at her, not taking his eyes of his opponent.

"And I could kill him right back," Evie snapped, her patience depleted.

Daniel waited, watching their conversation as if biding his time. Evie just wanted Julian safe. She kept a full eye on Daniel who did a slow dance, foot to foot, waiting for either Julian or Evie to make the next move.

"Wait. Daniel. This is not Julian's fight." Evie shouted the words hoping Daniel wouldn't turn a deaf ear just to spite her.

Daniel cackled and maintained his wary posture, eyes forever watching Julian. "Then tell him to be gone. You and I have to finish this fight. Now." His voice was low and dangerous and Evie sensed he was losing patience.

"No," Julian growled. "Stay back Evie, this is dangerous."

"I can handle it, Julian," she said She was beginning to tire of the lies.

"But, he will kill you." Evie heard the desperation in Julian's voice. He would let himself be killed if it meant saving her life.

"No, he can't kill me," she said softly. And in that instant she knew she'd already made a crucial decision. The deception ended now. "Julian, he can't kill me. For two reasons. One, I am trained to fight, with or without my sword. And two - I am a Nephilim. Nothing can stand in my way."

Evie thrust out her wings. A soft whirring echoed around her like the tumultuous flapping of a hundred hummingbird's wings. She rose two feet off the ground and hovered in a singularly majestic way that was hers and hers alone. Her wings glittered glossy white and silver behind her, rising high at her back, the highest point of its curve almost reaching the height of the ceiling of the cavern. It was clear that the Cavern was not made for a battling warrior angel.

Julian stood below her, too stunned to do much else besides stare at her in utter amazement. Evie met his eyes, and saw in its depths the hurt that she had put there. It answered the hurt she felt in her heart. She only hoped that someday he would forgive her.

For now though she needed to concentrate on Daniel, who had stood aside and watched her revelation as if it were an art house movie to be studied in depth. His sword still gleamed in his hand, like a living force filled with evil. The evil gleam matched his smile as he leered at her. Evie's gut hardened. Something was seriously wrong here. Why would Daniel be so sure of himself? What was he hiding? Evie was certain she had missed a vital clue, and with no time on her hands to reconsider what her instincts were telling her, she focused on the task of defeating Daniel.

Her opponent tossed his demonic sword between his hands again, as if it were too hot to hold within one grasp for long. Then he straightened to his full height and Evie's heart sank to the pit of her stomach.

She heard the dull whip and flap behind Daniel.

Wings, as white as the first snows, whiter the Evie's own wings, thrust out about him. The sound of his wings filled the Cavern, now overcrowded with two winged angels.

Evie's stomach twisted with horror as she absorbed the sight before her.

Daniel.

The angel, Daniel.

CHAPTER 9

*D*aniel's wings spread out behind him, impressive and dangerous, inspiring a little spark of fear in Evie's gut. He remained on the ground and regarded Evie as if considering his choices. She didn't see that he had many left at all. It was now a fight or die situation. And Daniel didn't give her the impression that he was about to back down. In fact he looked pretty confident.

Too confident.

Daniel. How had he lurked among the halls of Greylock all these years and managed to hide is angelic nature from everyone? Was angelic glamor that much more powerful than a Nephilim's? So powerful that none of the half-angels in the Brotherhood were unable to see through it?

Evie wished she'd listened to the screams of her instinct. Even her recollection of the strange vision of dying angels shedding rivers of glistening blood had not set off her alarms bells. Perhaps she'd been too occupied with thoughts of Julian and his mortality to pay attention to Daniel. She had underestimated him. And that was dangerous.

Daniel lunged toward her, swiping at her with his broad black sword. Evie ducked, paying more attention to the sharp edge of the weapon than what was going on around her.

THE CLATTER of hooves drew Julian's attention from the battle above him. Pollo came running into the Cavern, bearing a sword like a spear. Julian snorted at the sight of the faun trotting in hefting a weapon much taller than he was. Pollo leaned his body forward, balancing out the weight of the angelic sword but despite his compensation it still looked likely to tip him on his rear at any moment.

Julian gritted his teeth at the sight of Gavriel's sword, and instead of showing his attendant the appreciation he deserved, let out a bark of anger. "Pollo. What in Hades name are you doing?"

Pollo's eyes flicked to Julian's furious face, and his mouth quivered. "We had to bring him, Sire. He is our only hope."

"Where is he, Pollo?"

"Er . . . he is coming. He . . . needed his wings. "As he spoke Pollo's attention was drawn slowly away to the sight of the two angels clashing swords in the cavern above. His eyes grew wide with horror, flitting nervously between Daniel and Evie. When his gaze settled on her, Julian saw shock, admiration and hurt in the faun's eyes. Another person who judged her for her great omission.

Not that she didn't deserve it.

Julian broke Pollo's concentration as he spoke. "Pollo, no. You have no idea what you are doing."

The faun shook his head, short shark jerks to negate Julian's words. "He has promised to return to his cell after the battle, no matter what happens. The worst that can happen is he dies," Pollo added dryly. But Julian could tell it was an act. A slight twitch of his brow disclosed his utter fear of Julian's wrath.

But they were wasting time. And distracting Evie, which was

a dangerous thing considering the determined, dangerous angel she faced.

"What's going on?" she yelled down at Julian, daring to flick a glance at him before ducking another powerful blow.

Julian grabbed the sword from Pollo and tilted it up at her. Evie glanced at the sword and Julian could see her face pale as her gaze settled on the sword.

An angel's sword.

~

EVIE BLINKED at the sight of the weapon.

"No. He can't." Evie breathed hard trying to calm herself.

"That's what I've been trying to tell this imp of a servant," Julian hollered.

"And what I've been trying to tell you is that he has said yes and he is already on his way. Sire, if you choose to punish me you can do so afterward." Pollo thrust his shoulders backward, as if steeling himself for another barrage of remonstration from his ruler. When no scolding came he relaxed, but only slightly.

Evie, hovering above the furious Julian, snapped her attention back to Daniel who had circled her again. The span of his wings now turned the vast cavern space into a mere birdcage. A thrust of her own wings and Evie felt them brush against the sloping walls behind her. The space was too small to fight and fight well. Evie's heart thudded as she defended herself against another set of lunges. Tired of playing defense she knew she had to get on the front foot here.

Better get this over and done with.

Daniel moved left and Evie struck, her sword glancing off the angel's belt leaving a small slice of leather in its wake. He glared her then lunge at her, swirling his sword above his head, he grabbed the hilt with both hands and plunged it at Evie. If he'd hoped for a kill shot he was sorely mistaken. Evie, having seen the direction of the blow, had used the wall behind her to boost off, then somersaulted over Daniel's head to land behind him, unhurt.

Better get it over before Gavriel arrived.

His injuries would have already weakened him far too much. He'd be unable to withstand a battle with another angel. Especially an angel who looked to Evie to be infinitely stronger and much more confident than the damaged Gavriel.

Evie had last seen him a few hours ago. Would his wings have grown back to their full glory so quickly? Even so, his strength and stamina would surely have suffered from the intense pain of the removal of those wings. And considering the energy involved in reproducing those wings Evie wasn't confident in Gavriel's strength to fight any angel, let alone Daniel.

Daniel turned to face her, his fury twisting his face into something unrecognizable. Evie set her jaw, lifted her sword and charged at Daniel.

CHAPTER 10

*D*aniel was ready. He parried the shot, his face hard, jaw clenched. The defensive blow sent Evie tumbling to his right, slamming her headlong into the curved slope of the ceiling.

Daniel laughed, deep and arrogant, the sound echoing along the walls, taunting Evie. She set herself right, turning her attention back to him. She watched his body language, watched for the first opening. Daniel advanced, thrusting the sword at her, with his full weight behind the deadly weapon. Evie ducked, then dove below him. She was lighter, more nimble than Daniel, who didn't realize what she was about to do. Unable to stop his charge, Daniel smashed into the rock wall in front of him. His sword connected with stone and the sound the collision made was like thunder, only a hundred times louder. Evie wanted to cover her ears but realized the action would not ease the pain.

The sound rang both outside her ears and within her mind.

Evie winced, hoping the angel had injured himself severely. But he righted himself, barely flinching as he lifted the sword and turned his thunderous gaze back to her. He roared his anger. She felt it in her bones, in her muscles and behind her eyes as if her brain would explode. But she stiffened her resolve despite the ripple of fear that coursed through her. She reminded herself that she was angelic in nature too and that he was just a big bully.

But Daniel wasn't your average bully. Being an angel made him a bigger threat. But she wasn't about to let him off lightly. As he flew at her, she kept her eyes on him, ready to parry even his smartest side-swipe. Evie braced herself for impact.

Then she was rammed in her side by a force the size of a bus.

The impact sent her spinning off course, away from Daniel, and unable to right herself fast enough. She felt herself falling toward Julian, straight to the ground below. The shock of the blow caused Evie's wings to retract. Now wingless she fell faster and faster through the air. Her stomach tightened. There wouldn't be enough time to concentrate on bringing her wings back. Her last thought was whether or not Julian would bother to catch her. She'd seen the hurt and disappointment on his face when she had revealed her angelic nature. And she expected nothing from him.

Still ...

She closed her eyes and waited for the impact with cold hard stone. The next second, warm arms enveloped her, taking her full weight and halting her dead fall. Evie sighed and opened her eyes. She stared straight into Julian's worried eyes feeling slightly uncomfortable. She'd never been carried this way before, not since she'd grown into an adult. More importantly, not many people could bear the full weight of an angel. But Julian bore the mantle of a god, even if he was mortal right now. He held her gaze, a tiny spark of relief ran through her. Someday he would forgive her. Someday, when he had forgotten the pain of her betrayal.

She could deal with that.

"Well, well, well. Look what we have here." Daniel laughed, in the familiar yet condescending way of longtime friends with a history between them. Evie looked up, the tone of his voice making her worry for Gavriel who now hovered above them, his pearly white wings shimmering in the undulating light of the cavern. He'd been responsible for blindsiding her, and she wasn't sure she could forgive him anytime soon. Daniel's expression was far from kind. Hatred shadowed his eyes and his fist clenched the handle of his sword, harder, tighter. They had bad history. Then his lip curled in an angry sneer. "Where have you been for all these years, Gavriel?"

"Around." Gavriel's tone was sharp and short. It didn't sound like he wanted to indulge in idle chit-chat.

"I understand, Gavriel, I really do. You have been accommodated here in the realms of the underworld. A fair trade I would say. Better than Hell's hot arms wouldn't you agree?" Daniel closed the distance between himself and Gavriel, but remained just out of sword reach. Evie saw that Gavriel held the sword Pollo had brought with him. Now it didn't look so large at all. In fact it looked just right within Gavriel's hand.

And Gavriel himself had taken on an other-worldly glow.

"Stop showing off, Gavriel. We all know you still bear His Blessed Grace. But it won't scare me off. You are not invincible."

"Neither are you," came Gavriel's even response.

"But ... as I recall it is I who is stronger in body and in mind." Daniel gloated, the darkness in his eyes spreading thick through his eyes.

Gavriel's glow seemed to brighten, as he hovered before the dark angel. "Indifference does not equal strength, Daniel. It is a failing. Especially when it means you can so unfeelingly discard those who are your loved ones."

"Are you still on that rant, brother? Sorcha loved me, and I ... well I quite liked spending time with her." Daniel tilted his head, as if contemplating a thought. Then he asked, "Just what is love anyway?"

Gavriel's jaw tightened and Evie sensed a deep anger resonate from him. "You spent time with her and fathered a child on her.

And then you so willingly sacrificed both mother and child so easily. Your own flesh and blood? You would have destroyed your own child."

"Yes, yes, I know the story," said Daniel impatiently, made a rolling motion with his hand, urging Gavriel to be done with it. "I was there you know. And you had to butt in where you were not required. It was not your business to save them. It was your job to eliminate her and the half-breed."

"You mean your wife and your child?" Gavriel's said coldly. Evie strained to see his expression. She all but felt the pain in his voice that simmered beneath his anger.

"Does it really matter, brother?"

"Do not call me that. I am not your brother," Gavriel snapped at the dark angel.

"Even when you are forsaken you still think you are better than the rest, don't you?" Daniel scoffed. "Perhaps you need to be taught a lesson once and for all."

And then, as suddenly as the conversation began it ended.

The battle began.

Eve stood huddled next to Julian who watched the fight above them amazed at what they were witnessing.

A battle of Angels.

Only this one was much more personal than a painting on a church wall; personal to Evie who had grown to care for Gavriel. The angel had taken Patrick's place in way, with his advice and guidance. And now there was a distinct possibility that Daniel may well take another person from her. Evie stiffened, angry and afraid and feeling decidedly helpless.

"Hush," said Julian as Evie tightened her grip on his arm. "You are only half an angel. That makes you only half as strong as either of them. Don't even think you can make a difference to him in this fight."

"He's there because of me." Evie struggled against Julian's hold, glaring at him hotly.

"Not everything is about you, Evangeline," said Julian softly. And Evie supposed she deserved that little dig.

She sighed. "How can you say that when the only reason Gavriel is fighting that monster is because Daniel is here for the Seals?"

"There is much you do not know about Gavriel," Said Julian, his gaze still fixed above them. "Would you prefer to leave?"

"Not a chance," Evie snapped. Then she sighed. "I feel so helpless."

"He can handle it. So don't feel like you owe him anything."

"I thought you didn't want him to fight," she said dryly.

"I didn't want him to fight such a powerful angel when he's been chained in his cell for centuries. He isn't exactly in prime fighting condition."

Evie's attention remained on the hovering angels. Light flashed as their swords connected when they slashed and parried each other's blows. There was a strange rhythm to their battle, as if they knew each other well enough to predict the other's next move.

The battle was a dance.

A deadly dance.

a slashing sword connected with the cave wall and a small avalanche of rocks, dust and vicious stone chips rained down to the stone floor, narrowly missing Evie and Julian. They coughed and spluttered as they inhaled fine dust which floated on the air around them. Despite their discomfort they both peered through the screen of dust to watch the angels battling high above.

One good thing was that Gavriel's strength didn't seem in the least affected by his incarceration. He had his wings and he had his strength. And neither Daniel nor Gavriel seemed to tire and Evie soon began to wonder if they would fight until the cavern fell down around their ears.

"We can go on for a long time like this, Daniel. Just tell me what it is that you want and we can get this over with." Gavriel bit the words out been lunges as parries.

"I am here for the Seals of Hades, like I told the half-breed." Daniel nodded at Evie. "Too much time and effort has gone into locating the Seals for me to return empty-handed. You know how it is, brother," he said as he shrugged.

Gavriel snorted. "Well, this time you will have to return without what you came for."

"That is not an option." Daniel's words reverberated around the cavern. His voice contained a hard edge, an edge that seemed imbued with a dark power. Evie felt the evil in her bones and shuddered.

"Why do you need the Seals so desperately?" Gavriel asked, drawing away, just out of reach of Daniel's sword. "Of what importance could they possibly be to you? You are an angel and the Seals cannot be bestowed to a Heavenly being. The Seals themselves will not accept you as worthy to bear the Marks. You know that."

"Who said I would be the one to bear the Markings. I am not stupid, Gavriel. I have my plans."

"So, what? You intend to place a person of your choosing to possess the mark, a person whom will do your bidding? Ruling through another, Daniel? I did not think you would stoop so low."

"You are so narrow in your thinking, dear brother." Daniel laughed. "If you look at the big picture you will realize the vast power Hades has on this planet, the amount of resources that the Underworld controls. Resources that will or will not create chaos on the surface. Of course, that choice belongs entirely with Hades. Or whoever Hades is." Daniel smiled coldly.

"So your intent is to create mayhem using natural disasters?"

"That and more," Daniel responded impatiently. "The end of the world is long overdue, Gavriel. And it is past time that humans learned what it is like to reap the rewards of millennia of hatred."

"So you plan to kill millions of innocent people?"

"Gavriel, you have to understand. They are like flies. Insignificant. They have overrun the Earth and destroyed so much." Daniel shook his head impatient with his angel brother. "How is it that you do not see, brother?"

Gavriel shook his head, his brow furrowed with fury. "It is not our place to do this, Daniel."

"Your problem is you think too small, brother." Daniel laughed and sound was so loud Evie had to block her ears. "It is our duty to rid God's Earth of all pestilence. Including the half-breed. And I have a plan. I shall start with the Brotherhood."

Evie gasped and Daniel turned his eyes on her. "Yes, half-breed, you and your little half-demon friend will be the first ones I shall wipe from this earth."

Evie watched the two magnificent creatures engaged in furious mid-air battle. The air moved and she felt like she was dreaming. The scene before her was too real, too evocative. And it reminded her way too much of those strange death-filled images she'd seen while she stood at the threshold of Gavriel's cell.

Both Gavriel and Daniel were immensely strong, and sadly they also appeared to be equally matched. Muscles heaved and blood pounded amid the fury of beating wings and the clanging din of almighty swords. The ferocity of their combat was beyond anything Evie had ever seen. Beyond anything she was likely to ever see again.

The muscles in Evie's neck strained against the stress of staring heavenward for so long, but she remained so enthralled that despite the discomfort, she would continue watching as long as the battle lasted.

And that was another concern altogether. With their super-human stamina it was clear that both angels could battle for a long, long time.

Daniel growled, slamming his sword into Gavriel's. Sparks flew as he grunted, "The Seals, Gavriel." His words were ground through gritted teeth, spittle flying from his clenched jaw. "I want the Seals."

"They are not mine to give. Brother," Gavriel shouted above

the clamor of metal, spitting out the word 'brother' as if it were a live viper.

"Give them to me and I shall leave you in peace - or whatever peace it is that you can get down here among these creatures." Daniel sneered, eyes roiling blackness.

Gavriel swept his sword around him and aimed a blow straight at Daniel. The swords connected again with a resounding crash. As they connected, Gavriel shoved the dark angel back using the force of his momentum. "I cannot give them to you." He bit out as he pushed against the other angel.

"Why not?" Daniel shrieked, fury raising the veins in his face, mottling his cheeks with blood. "You will protect these ... humans?"

"The Seals have been taken." Gavriel circled, just out of reach from the deathly point of Daniel's ancient sword. "Another has been bound and will have to be released before you can have them."

"The Seals have been taken?" Daniel bellowed, his brow twisted in fury. "Why did you not tell me? Who has taken them? Who do I have to kill to claim the Seals?"

Gavriel glanced at Evie, and she saw his forehead crease with worry. He hung in the air, surrounded by swirling stone-dust. The fine particles floated around his body on eddies of air created by the bunched feathers of his wings.

With his head turned to Evie, he failed to see Daniel close in on him. But he must have felt the draft from Daniel's wings, or perhaps he heard the soft rush of feathers at his side. Either way he was too late. He could only stare, a look of confusion pulling his face into a white grimace as Daniel's sword pierced the flesh of his side.

Daniel hovered close to Gavriel, close enough that his face was an inch away from the injured angel. "Ah! I have you now, Brother. Though I shall not kill you." Daniels voice was a triumphant whisper which rang around the cavern and chilled the blood in Evie's veins. He shoved the sword deeper and said, "You must tell me where I can find the Seals, Gavriel. Or the point of this sword will be the least of your woes. I shall have to flay every inch of flesh from your bones." His voice was soothing, comforting and yet so threatening that Evie shivered.

Evie watched as blood spread, slick and red, along Gavriel's shirt. Unlike Daniel he wore no armor for protection. Her blood burned at the unfairness of this fight. It had been weighted in Daniels favor from the beginning. Protected by angelic metal, bearing that beautifully ghastly heavenly sword, he was a mighty opponent.

Impossible to defeat.

Evie's heart sank and an enormous weight seemed to bear down on her. A decision had to be made.

CHAPTER 12

*E*vie ears thrummed as she took a deep breath and stepped forward. "I have the Seals," she yelled, her voice shrill and almost hysterical. "Leave him alone and I'll give them to you."

Gavriel paid no heed having learned the danger of taking his eye off Daniel's sword. Daniel on the other hand stared at Evie from above, slowly comprehending what she said.

"You have the Seals?" he growled, his face black with fury.

Without a word, Evie thrust her sleeve up her arm, not caring that the fabric ripped at the seams. She bared the dark twisting markings of the Seals, and shook her arm up at the murderous angel.

With a crow of success, Daniel turned from Gavriel and flew at Evie, wings clamped tight at his back. His eyes glittered black and triumphant. Perhaps he'd intended to run her through with his sword or throw her down to the ground to struggle with her for the Seals. Perhaps he thought that killing her would mean he could claim possession of the Seals.

Evie never knew.

From the corner of her eye she watched Gavriel bear down

on Daniel, his face resolute and angry. Daniel's attention was focused on Evie who still held her arm up above her head. The swirling marks of the Seals were clearly visible, writhing and turning at the surface as if dark creatures lived within her golden skin. She took a fearful step backward, as terror coursed through her veins, but that was all the cowardice she allowed herself.

Gavriel charged headlong at Daniel, diving like an eagle at his prey. Quiet. Deadly. Precise. Daniel's attention remained focused on Evie's forearm. His eyes glowed with unadulterated lust. Even Angels fell victim to desire and the Seals were his obsession.

He'd put so many years of his life into obtaining them and now thought he would finally have them in his possession. Evie felt her fury rise at Daniels presumption. Who did he think he was? Just because he wanted the Seal's didn't mean he should get them. He seemed driven by his obsession and that was his undoing. He didn't see Gavriel coming at him from above. He didn't see the other angel raise his sword, the point facing downward as he descended. Nor did he see his Brother plunge the great sword into his ribs. Daniel went still as the sharp metal pierced his side, tore flesh and cracked ribs as it was thrust into his body. Only when he felt his body thrown did his attention shift from Evie's out-flung arm.

He hovered not far off the ground and swiveled his head, staring horrified at Gavriel just above him. "You have killed me?"

"No, not killed you." Gavriel shook his head regretfully. "Just stopped you from hurting Evie."

The dark angel pressed his hand to the wound, which pulsed rich warm blood between his fingers. His hand came away thick with blood and he studied it, perplexed. Evie frowned. Daniel seemed to be a powerful angel, beyond destruction, beyond even death. Why did he look like he was shocked to see his own blood. Or was it that he was more shocked that his 'brother' had drawn that blood from his flesh?

"I know you, Daniel. You would have killed her just to get a glimpse of the Seals." Gavriel's words broke Daniel's concentrated inspection of his bloodied hand. Then Daniel looked up.

"You know me well Brother," he admitted sadly as his body fell a few inches, his strength slowly failing him. "Why is she so important to you that you would slay your own brother to save her pathetic half-breed life?" He struggled to breathe as he asked the question, still studying Gavriel's face as if hurt but his actions.

"You have no idea how important she is. Or who she is." Gavriel clamped his jaw shut. Clearly he had been about to spill vital information to Daniel that he believed would be dangerous to Evie. She assumed he did not want to reveal to Daniel that they had developed a friendship, but she made a mental note to double check with him when this was all over. He'd bloody better survive to have that conversation if he knew what was good for him.

She was amazed that Gavriel had been so fortunate. That he had actually defeated the dark angel. Gavriel must have struck him deep because in the next moment Daniel lurched backward, and plunged the few yards remaining, landing on the stone floor with a resounding thump. He gazed up at Gavriel, a stunned expression on his face, his wings in disarray behind him.

No longer the mighty killer angel.

Gavriel grunted, hunched over with pain. His own wound had begun to sap his energy and he no longer had the strength to remain airborne. He slowly descended, while his great white wings shivered, creating various tiny hurricanes around the cavern. Evie watched in horror as he lowered himself until his feet touched the stone floor, then he crumpled into an unruly heap. But before she could run to his aid he raised his head, a determined expression on his face. He pushed himself to his feet and moved toward Daniel.

Gavriel had followed his opponent to the ground and now stood over him unmoving, his face inscrutable.

~

"GAVRIEL! HAVE YOU KILLED HIM?" She gasped as she ran to him. Evie threw an arm around him for support, though he barely leaned on her.

"No, he is not mortally wounded," Gavriel said resignedly. "He will be fully healed. Eventually."

Evie studied Gavriel's face, recalling the look of agony which had twisted his classic features when he'd sawn off his wings the evening she had first met him. Her gut wrenched as she realized he must be in the worst kind of agony. Those accursed bells of Heaven would be ringing in his head, causing him no end of pain. And yet he had paid it no mind while he fought to defend her life.

She should be grateful. Gavriel had just saved her life, but a tiny part of her had wanted to be the one to end his sorry life. Especially since he was responsible for Patrick's death. If he died he would deserve his end, for everything he'd done. For allowing his poor family to be killed. But was mere vengeance enough. Shouldn't he have to pay for what he'd done?

"Should we get him some medical attention?" She looked at the fallen angel as he lay crumpled on the ground. It was most certainly fitting that he lay right where he would be judged by the Gods.

Gavriel laughed and behind her she heard Julian's soft voice. "Daniel was trying his best to separate your head from your shoulders and here you are worrying about his health. Why should it bother you at all if I died right now?"

Evie considered Julian's question. Perhaps it was Daniel's angelic origin that pulled at her conscience. Not the best way to receive Heavenly blessing, killing an angel. But he had pulled the first punch. Infiltrated the Irin, guided Marcellus to use the Nephilim for his own purpose. He had come down to Hades to kill Evie. And he would have succeeded had Gavriel not saved her ungrateful ass.

The last thing Daniel deserved was Evie's pity.

"Guess he does deserve to be punished," said Evie still confused as to the words coming out of her mouth. She looked up to see both Julian and Gavriel staring at her, shaking their heads in disbelief while the subject of their conversation lay before them, all arrogance, pride and defiance.

"The great demon slayer is afraid of killing an angel?" Daniel stared up at her and laughed through his anger and pain. His eyes were a strange black, none of the whites visible.

At her side Julian stiffened at the words. A reminder that he was still sensitive to any mention of what she really was.

But Julian ignored the angel. "We have to get him to a cell. Pollo," Julian called the faun over his shoulder. "Get the guards to help you take him to Gavriel's cell. He shall remain there to await Judgment in the comfort and luxury befitting of his crime. And send word to the Gods that a case is at hand. I am sure they would want to dispense of Daniel as soon as possible. Within a few hours this angel will be residing in Tartarus."

Evie wanted to snort. The same comfort and luxury had been afforded to Gavriel whose crime certainly had not fitted his punishment. She followed Julian's gaze as he waited for Pollo.

But the faun hesitated and Evie saw the fear and trepidation in his eyes. He was very afraid of the heavenly creature, even in Daniel's injured state. Pollo hovered, the guards at his back mimicking his actions, clearly distressed.

Julian sighed wearily and bent to grab Daniel by the arm. The action caused Pollo and the guards to rush forward. Evie smiled to herself. Julian had just achieved his desire without ranting and raving at his disobedient servants. But Evie understood their fear. The angel instilled in her a similar dread, like a snake entwining its way along the bones of her spine.

She watched as the faun led the entourage away, their foot-steps echoing down the dark tunnel and away from the now ruined cavern. The once beautifully decorated space was now filled with broken columns. There were holes in the stone walls where swords had slashed chunks out of the once smoothed surface. Dust filled the air, hovering like a cloud.

The smoothed stone floor was veined with cracks in so many places it looked like an earthquake had just abused the cavern.

At that moment Cerberus howled, the long mournful sound echoing in triplicate along the tunnels. Fitting. It suited the feeling of mourning than settled over Evie like a heavy, unmovable weight.

CHAPTER 13

The Cavern emptied slowly as Julian left to check on Daniel, leaving just Gavriel and Evie alone and drained.

"I really think we should have your wounds looked at," said Evie, eying his blood drenched shirt.

The angel shook his head. "It will be fine. It is already healing." And when Evie studied the bloodstain she realized that very little of it shone fresh. She felt somewhat happier although not entirely confident in his health.

"Fine but if you do decide to keel over and die please ensure I am not around to see it. I don't think I can handle it right now." She spoke sharply but her voice didn't disguise her weariness.

"Do not worry, Evangeline. I will try my best to stay alive." Gavriel smiled and Evie studied his face. A countenance free of the lines and shadows of concern.

"What's wrong?" she asked him, her levels of patience at an all time low.

Gavriel seemed to sense she would not appreciate being given the runaround. He cleared his throat. "There is something you should know. I fear it will cause you much pain to hear this news but I believe I owe it to you to tell you the truth."

Evie's heart thudded. Was he about to tell her what she'd begun to suspect since she last spoke to him. Could he really be who she thought he was? Every fiber of her soul prayed that he was. "Tell me," she said leaning forward slight, eager to hear his words.

"It is about your father."

"Did you know him?" Evie figured she should play along, make it easy for him to get it all off his chest.

Gavriel stared at her for a moment. "Yes, I did know him. In fact I know him even now." Evie stopped herself from frowning. That was an odd thing for him to say if he was about to admit he was really her father. She felt a little drop of disappointment taint her happy expectation.

"What do you mean?" she asked, her throat tightening on the words. "Who is my father?"

"I have to warn you, Evie. You are not going to like it." Gavriel said, pausing to swallow hard. He pressed his fingers to his forehead and waited a moment. "Your father is an angel, that much is true. He is one of the fallen, very much like me. Cast out for spawning Nephilim on a human woman. The only difference with him was he felt little loss for the family he created, no remorse for his hand in their deaths."

Evie blinked. Memories of words filtered through to her.

She shoved the memories away. No. It was not what Gavriel was talking about.

Gavriel continued, unaware of Evie's inner struggle. "He had little regard for human life. His life revolved around himself and himself only." Gavriel sighed. "I am sorry Evie. I did not want to hurt you with this knowledge."

"You have told me nothing yet." She looked up at him, her expression hard as she mentally shut her ears to the words

"I fear it is more difficult for me than I expected. I have come to care a great deal about you Evangeline. As much as I would my own child. I do not wish to break your heart."

"Can you just tell me? I can take it." Evie was touched that he cared but he'd already broken her heart. He was not her father and nothing would make her feel better about that. "Who is my father, Gavriel?"

She tensed as Gavriel took a breath and spoke. "I am afraid it is Daniel." He didn't say anything more. And Evie just listened to the name of her father as it echoed in her ears over and over again, in a voice just like the dark angel too.

Words floated to Evie.

Sorcha loved me, and I ... well I quite like spending time with her... Just what is love anyway?

It was not your business to save them. It was your job to eliminate her and the half-breed.

You mean your wife and your child?

Does it really matter, brother?

Mocking laughter followed and Evie jerked out of her shock, looking around, searching the cavern for Daniel.

"And how did I end up with Patrick?" she asked although she already suspected she knew.

"I took you to Patrick and left you in his care."

"Did you tell him who my father was?"

"I didn't have time. He assumed you were mine but I didn't have the time to correct him." He fell silent and Evie couldn't think of a response. She just stared at the far wall, studying a fresco shattered to pieces.

She must have been silent far too long as Gavriel cleared his throat and asked, "Are you alright, Evangeline?"

Evie glanced at Gavriel having half forgotten he was still there, still waiting, still concerned how she would take the news.

"Don't worry, Gavriel. I am fine. I am not going to fall apart on you."

"I am very glad."

Evie nodded. "Right now I think I need a rest. Now that your cell is occupied where will you go?"

"That is a good question. I will go and find out." Gavriel began to walk off, then stopped to glance back at Evie, his eyes filled with concern. "Are you going to be alright? I know it is not what you wanted to hear."

Evie managed a weak smile. "I will be fine. He may be my father but he has no claim on me apart from a genetic one. I feel nothing for him."

Gavriel gave Evie one last look, then turned and left her to her thoughts.

She'd lied. She didn't feel nothing for Daniel.

What she felt was fury and a deep-seated need for vengeance.

EVIE RETURNED TO HER ROOM, her mind filled with thoughts of Daniel and Gavriel, thoughts that she didn't want swimming around in her head right now.

She pushed the door open to find her two friends on the sofa laughing over some obscure joke. When Evie entered they fell silent but it was her face that was their cause for concern.

"Evie." Ling rose and came to Evie as she reached the foot of her bed and found she could go no further. Evie sank onto the bed. "What's wrong? What happened?"

Ash hurried over and sat beside Evie. "Eves. What's the matter?"

Evie took in a shuddering breath. "You two need to get back to the estate ASAP."

"Why?" Both girls asked in unison.

"Because, Daniel came to Hades and had a huge fight with one of the Angels here."

"There's an angel here in Hades?"

"Daniel's here?"

Evie held up her hands. "One question at a time," she said as she sighed. "Only one question allowed at a time please." Evie fell onto her back, enjoying the feel of the soft mattress beneath her aching back.

"Okay," said Ling. "Talk."

Evie cleared her throat. "Daniel came to Hades to get the Seals. Then he wanted to fight me but Gavriel wouldn't allow it so they had this all out battle in the Cavern. Then Daniel was about to kill Gavriel for the Seals and I told him I had it so he wanted to kill me. So Gavriel stabs him and they threw him in Hades." Evie turned over, closed her eyes and snuggled her pillow. "Man, I need some rest."

The girls were silent. Too silent.

Evie cracked open one eye to find both Ling and Ash standing in front of her, arms folded. "What?" she asked although she suspected she already knew what they were thinking.

"How do you get yourself mixed up in stuff like this?" asked Ash shaking her head.

"No idea. Wish I knew so I could avoid it." Evie sighed again. "You two must go back home. Who knows what the brotherhood is doing without their Master and without Daniel. You have to tell them what happened."

"Fine. But we're coming right back." Ling's voice was calm, reasonable and brooked no argument.

But it didn't matter to Evie. Right now her friends had to get out of Hades. The Brotherhood needed them more than Evie did. "No. Go and take care of things there. I have a few loose ends to tie up and then I'll be on my way back. Oh, and you must take Castor with you."

"He's not going to like it," said Ling.

"He doesn't have a choice," Evie said firmly. They both stared at her for a moment. "What?"

"Should we go now?" asked Ling, with an almost petulant pout.

"That would be for the best."

"Fine," said Ling as Evie swung her feet to the floor and rose to hug the girls. "Evie, you must take care of yourself. Promise us that you won't do anything risky?"

"I promise."

"Or stupid?" asked Ash.

"I promise."

"Do you believe her?" Ash asked Ling, raising and eyebrow.

"I never believe anything she says," Ling responded, giving Evie a dirty look.

Evie laughed. "Get going you two." She grabbed them each by the arm and dragged them to her door. "Ask Pollo to fetch Castor and don't let him convince you to leave Castor behind. I want all of you home. Castor would do better tending what few patients he still has. He needs to make himself useful." Evie sensed her argument may be weak but she realized that between the walk from the Cavern to her rooms, she'd made the decision to go to Tartarus and see Daniel face to face. Which meant she wasn't going to be around the palace for a while. Seemed pointless having her friends here, hanging around and waiting for her return. They were better off doing their jobs.

At the door the girls nodded solemnly then headed off down the passage. In the end the Nephilim always did what was needed, despite their personal opinions.

Once the door closed Evie's world returned to its recent state of shatter and ruin.

She eyed the bed, then stalked to the hot pool, tugged off her boots and tore off her clothes. She slid into the steaming hot water and leaned against the edge of the pool. Heat rose off the surface and Evie released a sigh that came from somewhere deep within her soul.

CHAPTER 14

*E*vie was about to step into Julian's study when she caught movement just inside the door. From where she stood she could see Persephone slink into the room mere seconds ahead of Evie. The goddess took a seat beside Julian, a contemplative smile on her face. Julian's jaw clenched tight as he examined her face, his fingers clenching tightly on the small leather-bound book in his hand.

Now what does she want? That smile could only mean she had some plan whirling about in that twisted brain of hers.

Julian had far too much on his mind to be distracted by the goddess.

Persephone took a deep, husky breath and reached over to pat Julian's thigh. "Julian, Julian. What are we going to do about you?"

"What do you mean?" he asked, taking hold of her hand by her slim wrist and moving it off his leg. He dropped her hand back into her own lap, then opened the book onto his legs. Sef's face lost a few shades of color. "I don't have time for your games, so speak or leave."

"Ooh," she breathed, ignoring his recent insult. "So very harsh with your consort, dear one."

Julian snorted. "You and I, and not to mention the entire population of Hades, know very well you are not and never were my consort Persephone. What are you up to?"

"Me?" she asked, feigning innocence. Evie noted she feigned it too well. "I'm not up to anything. All I'm concerned with now is the hold that girl has on you."

"It is not a hold on me, it is a hold on the throne of Hades. Would you prefer she become the ruler, then? How would you like to be her consort?" Julian smiled at Persephone as he asked the question and Evie was sure he enjoyed putting that question to the goddess.

"That is preposterous and you know it." Persephone spoke with the ice of winter and yet a little tremor belied her nerves.

"Not preposterous at all. Should Evangeline keep the throne then by her right as Hades you shall be her consort. And as per the terms of your marriage you are beholden to her in every way as you would be to your husband."

Persephone's face had now lost all color and Evie was enjoying her reaction as much as Julian was. "I will never allow that to happen." She spat the words at Julian. "I have my ways. I can get rid of her if I wanted to."

"Not while she has the Mark." Julian smiled, speaking softly, almost lovingly he said, "And not if you want to reap the consequences. Touch one hair on her head and you will have me to deal with."

The temperature in the room dropped to below Arctic despite the crackling fire.

Persephone rose stiffly and headed for the door. When she saw Evie standing there her eyes glittered, hatred clear in her vicious stare. The goddesses didn't miss a step, moving straight toward Evie, and brushing past as she stormed off down the tunnel. Evie stared after her, wondering what had gone wrong in the cosmos to turn Persephone so nasty.

When Evie turned to face the door she saw Julian watching her. His face was inscrutable.

She forced herself to enter the room and head to the sofa directly opposite him. A part of her was a little afraid to be too near him. Afraid to feel his rejection. She drew in a shuddering breath and pushed those thoughts out of her head.

When she sat she placed her hands on her lap and studied them. "I'm so sorry." Julian examined her face, his eyes dark. She'd hurt him with her secrets and wondered now if she was too late. "I wanted to tell you the truth, but I never found the right time. It's just seemed like something too hard to discuss."

"Why would the truth be too hard?" he asked, his tone still holding an edge of ice that stabbed at Evie's heart.

"Before I entered Hades, I was told not to reveal my species. That being a Nephilim in the Underworld was dangerous in itself. And when I received the Seals I assumed that a Nephilim bearing the Seals would be more dangerous."

Evie paused for a moment, then swallowed as Julian closed his book and placed it on the arm of the sofa. "You could have trusted me, Evangeline." There was a hint of accusation in his voice that Evie understood. She'd feel the same way if she were in his place.

"I'm sorry. There was never a right time." The shadows shifted on the planes and hollows of his face, but his expression did soften. It gave Evie hope. "Can you forgive me?" she asked hopefully.

Julian shifted so he was facing her. "I would think that we should be able to resolve any issues between us." He leaned forward and ran a hand along her cheek. Evie suppressed a shiver. "We have … something. I'm not sure what it is yet but I care for you. More than I have cared for anyone in a very long time. I don't want to lose that. But I do need to know that I can trust you."

Evie nodded, her heart beating wildly. "You can trust me. And this thing ..." she moved her hand between Julian's chest and hers. "These feelings ... they mean a lot to me. And I don't want to lose it either. There's just so much going on right now."

Julian nodded. "I know. Nothing's easy right now, is it." He smiled.

A moment passed that felt strangely comfortably and a little too domestic for Evie's liking. She looked at her hands again and cleared her throat. "I want to see Daniel," Evie said softly. She didn't look up at Julian. She knew she'd see those dark eyebrows raised, disbelief and exasperation in those beautiful black eyes. She was pretty sure she felt his tension thickening the air easing through the space between them like a winter cold front.

Dead silence greeted her.

Evie looked up slowly, steeling herself to face him. Julian's eyes glittered, anger accenting both coal-black orbs. "You must be insane." The words were clipped and cold, sending ripples of hurt deep into Evie's heart.

She gazed at him, and hesitated. Then she took a deep breath and said, "I have to see him, Julian. Please try and understand." She paused. Swallowed. "He is my father."

Julian paled. "Who told you this?" His tone was harsh and disbelieving.

"Gavriel. He told me the truth after they took Daniel to his cell."

Julian was silent for a long time. A nerve throbbed at his temple, his eyes grew darker. There was no way to tell what he was thinking and Evie didn't dare to ask.

At last he answered. "Father or not, do you really believe it's worth the effort. He didn't exactly seem the loving father type to me. Especially when you recall that he wanted to kill you." His voice came out harsh, grating.

"No," Evie said slowly, pain fisting within her chest. "No, I don't think he would want to see me. I don't really think he would care either way."

"Then why do you want to do this to yourself?"

"Because all my life I wanted to find the angel who was my father. I spent my life thinking he was an angel called Gabriel. And when I met Gavriel and learned of his past and got to know him better, a small part of me hoped it was him. It should have been Gavriel. It should have." Evie's voice broke as she sank against the back of the couch and rested her head in her hands. That head felt too heavy to hold up. Suddenly, Evie rose and paced the floor, rubbing her palms against her pants. "It should have been Gavriel," she whispered to herself. Julian would hear her pained words but she didn't care. He didn't move, didn't say anything. He seemed to sense that despite her pain, Evie wouldn't want hugs and soothing words. And he was right. She needed strength.

Evie stopped pacing and looked at Julian just as he looked up. "I have to see him face to face. Tell him who I am. I want him to answer for my mother's death." Evie's eyes shone, moist with a kaleidoscope of anger and grief.

"I still don't think it's a very good idea, Evie." Julian shook his head. "Tartarus is a dangerous place. And the way there is treacherous."

She shrugged. "I'll have your blessing, the King's blessing."

Julian sighed, frustration furrowing his brow. He scrubbed his head, mussing his hair. And Evie smiled, though she hid the happy expression. Julian could wring a smile from her on her bleakest day. His fingers sent his hair poking off into twenty different directions; quite endearing actually.

Too endearing.

"Then let Gavriel come with me-"

"Where is Gavriel going with you?" Gavriel walked in the study, crisp white shirt tucked into a pair of dulled black leather trousers. He pulled off the look, managing to exude a calm that Evie knew was a mere facade. The sharp jut of his jaw below his left ear, and the stiff rise of his shoulder confirmed he was still in pain. Naturally his physical agony would have disappeared to where-ever it was that archangels sent their pain - unlike mere Nephilim who healed slower and hurt longer.

"To Tartarus," Evie said, staring at his face, her own bright with defiance.

"No, no, no, no, no." Gavriel shook his head while wagging his finger at her remonstrating at her as he spoke each 'no'. "Tartarus is no place for Nephilim. Dangerous... fire....Lots of mean and ugly prisoners."

Evie huffed. "Stop making fun of me - this is serious."

"What? You really want to go to Tartarus? Next you will be saying you want to speak to Dan..." he trailed off staring at her as if she had grown two heads more grotesque than poor Cerberus.

Evie folded her arms and raised an eyebrow while Gavriel's jaw tightened, the muscles of his neck taut. He didn't like it but that was his choice.

"Evie's insisting on meeting with him. I don't think it's a good idea." Julian now stood at the mantelpiece, and stared at the flames behind the grate, as if they would jump out and bite him if he dared blink.

"I have to go. And I told you why." Evie folded her arms her shoulders tight. Then she faced Gavriel, her eyes narrowed. "And how come Gavriel's walking around a free man if he's supposed to be in his cell, paying for his sins?" She hadn't meant to sound ungrateful but she found it odd that he suddenly seemed to have the run of the place.

Julian cleared his throat. "Gavriel has done Hades a great service. He saved your life and the Seals from Daniel. I thought he deserved a small reprieve. And I've discussed it with the Council of Judgment- they agree."

"So he will return to his prison eventually?"

"Evangeline, you sound like you want me back in my cell?" Gavriel teased but she didn't even look in his direction.

Julian nodded and Evie realized she didn't like the idea very much. "I don't think its fair."

"To be honest, I agree. But there is little that I can do about it. Unless Gavriel escapes I have to send him back to his prison." A wave of ice dashed into Evie. Escape? Was that what Julian and Gavriel had planned? If so she wasn't going to disagree. Gavriel didn't belong in an eternity of Hell even if he'd been relegated to Hades and not the burning depths of Tartarus.

Evie nodded, then turned her thoughts back to her current task. "So when can I leave? Am I allowed to fly? Can you show me a map or something so I can find Tartarus?"

"You are insane." Gavriel was fairly vibrating with anger. His face had taken on a distinctly uncomfortable shade of blue. Evie swallowed. "Why in Heaven's name would you want to even talk to him? He tried to kill you. Would have killed you if I had not stopped him."

"Don't you think I know that?" Evie asked, her eyes icy? "But I do need to see him face-to-face. Say my piece. And I need answers."

Gavriel regarded Evie, his forehead contorted in a scowl, as if attempting to solve the puzzle of her craziness. "Why are you doing this to yourself, Evangeline?"

"Can't you understand that it's something I need to do? He let my mother die. He left me for dead. He killed Patrick. He has to be held accountable."

"That's what Tartarus is for," said Julian wearily. "He will get his punishment."

Evie sensed she was going nowhere fast. Neither man would relent.

She gritted her teeth, impatience making her fingers curl into fists. Julian was in charge, she would give him that. But, Evie had one last card to play. "If you don't allow me to see Daniel I will not release the Vows of Ascension. That way I will be Ruler and no-one can stop me from seeing him," she finished carefully, knowing her words would hit home. Hard.

Both men stared at her, flabbergasted at her audacity.

Gavriel shook his head.

Julian just blinked.

The room fell into an ominous silence. Neither men would appreciate being pushed into a corner but Evie had the upper hand. And they both knew it. Julian's jaw tightened.

"Evie, I only want to protect you, but if it means that much to you then I can't object. You are, as the New Ruler, in control. You may do as you wish." From the look on his face those words must have been very hard to say. He looked stiff as if he was trying to keep his emotions out of his expression. He took a breath before saying, "Gavriel should accompany you though. Having been there before, Gavriel knows the way."

"Thank you," was all Evie could manage.

Julian nodded abruptly. "When do you wish to leave?"

"I have a little less than two weeks left of my decision time. The sooner we leave and return the sooner we can get the Ascension Ceremony completed."

"Do you know how long it will take you to get to Tartarus? The route is treacherous, thus making the trip longer."

"That's why I have Gavriel," Evie cut in quickly, still sensitive about mentioning her true nature to Julian. Gavriel nodded.

Julian, outvoted, acquiesced. He rose and walked to Gavriel. "Unfortunately, it is not as easy as going straight to Tartarus. You will need to meet the Gods of Judgment and obtain permission." Then Julian turned to face Evie, his brow furrowed. "Should the gods request you to perform a task, you do so at your own peril. Understand that there is nothing certain about entering the prison of uncountable souls of evil."

Evie nodded. Nothing she heard him say had done anything to change her mind.

Julian turned to Gavriel. "And Gavriel?" The archangel looked at the king of the underworld a curious expression to his face. His features tightened when Julian spoke. "If she is hurt I will hold you responsible."

Gavriel nodded. "I will guard her like my own kin, Julian. You need not doubt my intentions. She is like my very own child."

Evie and Gavriel left the room. Only the sound of their heels on the softened moss-carpet broke the silence of the halls.

CHAPTER 15

*E*vie and Gavriel picked their way down a rock path outside the warren of black tunnels that was the royal palace. The path that would take them to the Temple of Judgment. Gavriel seemed to know his way around, moving down passageways unerringly until he reached the exit that led to the pathway. Evie hung back a little and refrained from asking him any further questions. He still gave off an aura of seething anger, although it had simmered down a few notches from potent fury.

So he was angry that she wanted to see Daniel.

That was really his own problem - it had nothing to do with Evie. In fact, the way she saw it, it was all a bit of Gavriel's fault anyway. If it hadn't been for him she wouldn't be alive. And it was with his falsehoods that he'd given her to Patrick to raise. His lies, which she had been brought up on.

What a sham! To grow up worshiping a man who wasn't really yours to worship. Evie wanted so desperately to destroy every particle of Daniel's blood which ran in her veins. But she couldn't deny her parentage any more than she could deny her wings. She sighed.

Daniel was just her sire.

That was all he was to her. All he would ever be.

Now she followed Gavriel as he led her lower and lower into the bowels of Hades. They followed a gritty path peppered with shards of fine black stone and uneven black gravel. A tiny river of molten lava hugged their gritty path. The angry stream spat red sparks of super-heated rock as it traveled lazily beside them. Heat licked at her, from her thigh to her arms to her cheeks. Beads of perspiration dotted her skin, running down her spine until she felt a wet patch at the waistband of her pants.

Gavriel walked on, unaffected. No sweat, no discomfort, not even the slightest sheen of cession on his angelic forehead. Coarse black sand rustled beneath their feet. Gleaming black rocks littered their path, slowing them down as they made their way around the obstacles. Evie slid left, the incline to the fiery river a little too steep for comfort. She scrambled up the steep rise sending a fall of rocks splashing into the molten stream, wishing she could just fly where they needed to go.

Then Gavriel took a sharp right, and Evie gasped.

The path rose, up a steep incline, bordered by twenty foot rock plinths. Lights flickered beyond the path, shivering shadows beckoned.

"Is that the Temple of Judgment?" asked Evie.

"No. It is merely the entrance to the path. It is a long way," said Gavriel before he hurried off.

Gavriel and Evie followed the path in silence, not even their feet daring to break the peace and quiet. A small mountain blocked their path, split by a set of stone steps cut out of the ebony, grey-streaked rock-face. The path glowed, lit by red flames reaching and twisting from iron torches fixed to the walls.

Evie titled her head, following the path further up ahead. At the peak of the mountain sat a small temple. A few columns had pitched over, spilling broken white stone across torn marble tiles. The gleaming columns that remained standing tilted precariously, threatening to topple over any second. The gods of this tiny temple was surely nowhere to be found. The place felt forsaken, the dull ache of it echoing in Evie's gut.

In silence they began their climb, avoiding the cracks in the steps. It didn't take long for them to reach the top of the steep staircase. Gavriel stopped before her and Evie moved forward to get a better look. The center of the black marble floor rose and fell, ripped open by an enormous crack, as if the ground had decided it didn't like the ancient Greek architecture, then decided half-way through it wasn't worth the effort.

The gash in the floor snaked ahead, veining into the dark depths of the temple. They followed as the crack grew into a gaping maw, and followed even further until they saw how it ended; into a deep, bottomless ravine.

Evie glanced up at Gavriel. "Now what?" Gavriel raised an eyebrow and nodded in the direction of the shadowy pit.

"That's where we're headed?" She asked eying the pit dubiously. "Does it even go anywhere?"

Gavriel snorted. "Come Evangeline, we'd better get going." He thrust his wings into the darkness surrounding them. They hovered above him, almost disembodied in the thick blackness. Evie sighed and shucked her own wings out.

"Is there any other way in?" she asked hopefully, recalling Baaruk's warning about angels in the underworld.

"Sorry Evie. This is it." He rose off the ground and glided over the edge, hovering over the gaping pit.

Evie swallowed as ripples of fear undulated through her gut. She clenched her jaw shut. If Gavriel thought it was the best way then who was she to disagree.

With wings fluttering and sending wavelets of hot air surging around them, Gavriel and Evie descended, further into the belly of Hades. Down there somewhere within those fiery depths was Tartarus.

~

THE DARKNESS WAS SURREAL. Evie had never before experienced the utter lack of light which greeted her as she sank deeper into the gaping maw of the earth. She wasn't afraid, just disconcerted by the sheer blackness around her. She wasn't comfortable with being unable to see where she was going. Soon, the faint glow of Gavriel's wings below her caught her frantic eye.

She breathed a sigh of relief, reaching out so that her fingertips traced the rock wall as they dropped lower and lower. They didn't speak much during their descent.

What could they talk about? Why he lied to Patrick about being her father? A lie by omission is still a lie. Why he'd saved her? Besides, conversation itself was difficult in the dark. All she had to do was hover and lower herself a little at a time.

Mostly they fell slowly. And it was the slow part that was hard. Left alone in the dark with just her thoughts for company was not a healthy thing for Evie, not right now, when so many facets of her world were tumbling down around her feet.

She cleared her throat. "Gavriel?"

From below his voice rose, disembodied and strange, and sharp. "Pay attention to the walls of the hole Evie, they are dangerous. One wrong move and you could be seriously hurt. Here in the Underworld both our abilities to heal are slowed to an almost human rate. You won't die, but you would jeopardize your chances of reaching Tartarus." That was all he said. Then he fell into silence again and Evie figured there was no point in talking to him again if he was going to bite her head off like that.

Her entire life had taken a turn for the crazy. Julian's beautiful face had touched her heart. He'd been angry, and disappointed in her. Of course, he would be. Lies did that to people. He would forgive her with time. He seemed like he'd wanted it to work out between them.

Before she'd entered the Underworld, Baaruk, the albino demon friend she'd made had been adamant that Evie keep her angelic identity a secret. Adamant that her very life depended on that secrecy. She had trusted his advice and rightly so. Persephone would have had a field day with that information given that she'd already tried to terminate Evie once during her stay in Hades.

Right now she had to concentrate on what she would say once she met her father. Evie shuddered. She bit her lip, pressing into the soft flesh. Seeing him, meeting him face to face, it was the right thing to do. She was sure if it. The air moved hot and angry around her, ruffling her hair and throwing strands around with wild flair.

Truthfully, she was being selfish. This was all about Evie.

She wanted to look into his eyes when she told him who she was. She wanted to see his reaction, to know for herself what he thought of her revelation. Perhaps she would see some flicker of regret or remorse in those eyes.

Evie shook her head. No, she wasn't going to see Daniel for a family reunion. She just wanted him to be accountable. To acknowledge he was responsible for her mother's death. It was better than leaving Hades without any sort of closure.

She gritted her teeth. Again, the memory of Daniel walking the halls of Greylock for this past decade, twisted within her like a hot knife. She'd been face to face with him countless times in the last few years. But, that was the strangest thing- face to face and never the slightest knowledge or awareness of who he really was.

Without Gavriel's angel light - *anjelo lumino*, they would have seen nothing below them. Maybe they would have seen the eerie vein-thin lines of red lava within the rock-face, but that would have been where their ability to see would have ended.

The point of the depths of hell was to be as dark as the depths of hell. Evie's lips curled into a small smile. Until she remembered where she was.

Gavriel lit their way revealing the reality of the tubes shape and design. It did not descend straight down into the earth. It curved and twisted in a cruel and ungainly fashion. As if some molten snake had slithered its way deep into the core of the earth, twisting and turning as it went.

Resigned, Evie lowered herself after Gavriel in silence.

AFTER WHAT SEEMED like hours had gone by, Evie heard Gavriel speak. "Hold up there, Evangeline," He called as he slowed down. He'd finally stopped his rapid descent. Evie lowered herself faster until she was level with Gavriel. He turned and regarded her with his hooded eyes.

"I hate to sound like a ten year old, but how much further? We've been going at this pace for hours now," Evie asked. She suspected she already knew the answer. It can't be an easy place to get to - not the best spot for a vacation.

"A while more. Perhaps you should ask less questions and think more on what you are going to say to your - to Daniel." His voice was edged in bitterness.

Evie grunted silently.

CHAPTER 16

*E*vie gritted her teeth, biting her tongue on the words which teetered at its edge. Gavriel, was infuriatingly quiet. Gavriel. Should she now call him by his rightful name - The Archangel Gavriel? Or was it better to just continue as if he was still Gabriel, the father she had thought was hers but whom she never truly had?

Heat rose up from below Evie's feet, seeping through the thick soles of her boots. The further they sank into the belly of Hades the hotter it became. Sweat dripped from Evie's brow and trickled down her back as she went down, down, down. Below her Gavriel was unaffected by the heat. No perspiration dampened his brow, nor did his shirt stick to his body like limp seaweed. Evie snorted, reminded that she had only received the gifts of flight and glamor. Her search for her only living relative was meant to result in connecting with her family and finding out more about herself. Seems like she pretty much owned the short straw throughout her life, then. She huffed silently, it would not pay to alert Gavriel to her little pity-party.

The heat now burned her skin, as if she stood mere inches away from a blazing fire. Evie glanced around. The tunnel through which they now sank was lined with oily, black rock. Red veins of lava gleamed in tiny tributaries within the rock-face. They moved like skinny caterpillars, glowing bright and hot in squiggly lines set deep within the black glistening rock. Beauty in Hell, thought Evie. Who would have thought that possible?

The trip had taken the better part of the day, and Evie didn't feel like they'd made much progress though, considering they were hovering rather than flying down the rock tube.

Sinners were hurled down this tube, sent falling to their eternal punishment. Falling down this pitch black hole would be punishment enough for Evie, considering it wasn't exactly a wide space. Evie shuddered and shivered. In her mind's eyes she saw a punished soul falling in the darkness, hitting and bouncing off the rock-faces with every bend and turn of the tunnel. A person would be seriously damaged by the time they reached the bottom. If not seriously dead. But they'd be dead before they got here ... Evie frowned in confusion then put the thoughts out of her head.

The heat battered her hard. Immortal or not, the heat that could certainly have melted the feathers off her wings considering she wasn't as powerful as an Archangel. Flying too fast toward the heat would allow the molten air to penetrate her silken feathers to the tender skin covering the bones of her wings. In all its elegant and angelic glory, a Nephilim's wings were still a biological structure, functioning not much different to the wings of a bird. A slower descent prevented the heated air from reaching the skin where feather met pore, where the feathers could melt right off their wings.

Gavriel, straight-backed and silent, showed no sign of tiring on his reluctant journey. Heat burned her already parched skin, drying out her eyes and making it difficult to blink. Even her throat was gritty and sand-paper-like. Swallowing did nothing to moisten her mouth and throat. The heat seemed to suck every drop of moisture from her entire body. She was breathing hot air- in and out as if she was within the heart of a volcano.

At last Gavriel slowed his pace to a stop and Evie lowered herself to him. The hole had widened enough to allow Evie to reach eye-level with him. And to see that they had reached the ground, not a few feet below her heels.

They dropped to the stone floor and Gavriel walked off, leaving Evie to hurry after him. Casting desiccated eyes around she confirmed what her instinct had been insisting. They were standing beside a pool of boiling lava that spat and spluttered red molten rock.

Evie blinked, and was surprised that her eyelashes and eyebrows weren't singed off her face by now. A tortured howling scream echoed on the darkened air, the sound twisting and turning around her. Evie did not scare easily. She killed demons and bad guys for a living. But that scream scraped a sharpened nail along a deeper visceral nerve, bringing a cold film to her skin.

She stayed close behind Gavriel. He seemed invulnerable here. Head held high, so sure of himself in a place no angel should ever set foot. In the distance, scorched mountains rose, hiding the black valley from whatever it was that lay beyond.

To their right rose a hill. A man made his way up the incline, bare feet streaked with blood as they slipped against polished black sand. His arms bulged, muscles quivering as he pushed an enormous boulder up the mountain, and struggled to maintain his footing. His body was covered with a film of moisture, whether from his exertions or the current climate of Tartarus it didn't matter.

He grunted as he pushed, a vein at his temple throbbed threateningly as the boulder moved a foot, then two. Then it stopped and so did the man, who turned around, supporting the rock at his back with his body as he rested. His face was over-grown with a beard as long as he was tall. A beard which hid skin darkened by smudges of soot and black sand. He dragged a muscle-bound arm across his forehead, re-distributing the soot on his face and wiping off the beads of sweat which had collected there. The man sighed and turned to face his burden. The muscles in his limbs bunched and the veins on his arms distended as he pushed the rock again.

"Don't make a sound." Gavriel spoke softly, clearly loath to disturb the poor man. The empathy in Gavriel's face was enough to shut her up. So she kept her silence and watched.

As the man turned his head, Evie caught a glimpse of his eyes. In those grey orbs she saw despair, exhaustion, hopelessness. She gasped at the anguish painted clearly upon his strained features. He hissed as he breathed out, pushing with all his might, the vein at his temple throbbing harder. At last, after what seemed an eternity, the man reached the summit and sank to the ground, the muscles in his arms and legs quivering with exhaustion.

After a few minutes he rose, casting his eyes about for something, one arm supporting the rock. Just then the ground trembled. And with it the boulder. It rolled back and forth, rocking with the quake. That was all it took for the rock to be sent over the edge and roll, ever faster down the hill. At the peak, the man stared helplessly after the tumbling rock, tears of despair filling his slate-like eyes.

He made a slight motion with one shoulder that Evie would have thought was a tired impression of a shrug, then made his way down the hill, resignation bowing his shoulders and thinning his eyes. At the foot of the hill he faced the boulder like an opponent in battle, steeling himself as he began to push the boulder back up the hillside.

"Why is he doing that?" Evie could no longer contain her curiosity and spoke in hushed tones.

"Do you not know who he is?" Gavriel raised an eyebrow. When Evie shook her head he continued, "That is Sisyphus, who for his arrogance has been punished with pushing this boulder up that hill for all eternity. And for all eternity, as soon as he reaches his destination, the boulder will be sent rolling back down the hill for him to repeat his task."

Evie was slack jawed. "Harsh."

"It pays never to be arrogant toward the gods then, doesn't it?" Gavriel countered. Evie wanted to counter with her current opinion of the gods but thought it best to keep quiet given her current location.

They left Sisyphus to his eternal punishment and walked on. Gavriel skirted a bubbling lava pool and strode toward a cave just ahead. The entrance rose before them like the black mouth of some evil monster. The edges of the entry-way were even trimmed with sharp stalactites, huge terrifyingly sharp teeth from a nightmare best forgotten. A cacophony of shrill screams and hopeless moans rose and fell within the warren of caves as they stepped inside the evil mouth. The sound echoed back and forth so mournfully it raised the hairs on Evie's neck.

Evie leaned toward Gavriel and asked softly, "So where do we find him?" It wasn't as if the corridor of black rock was marked with room numbers in fluorescent red.

Gavriel walked ahead in silence, and Evie clenched her jaw shut. He didn't want her here so he certainly wasn't going to make things easy on her. Best to just leave things as they were. The last thing she wanted to do was piss him off badly enough for him to change his mind and take her right back to Hades. This needed to be done and soon.

Before she lost her nerve.

CHAPTER 17

Gavriel led Evie through another warren of passageways, so similar to those of Hades palace, and yet so different. The heat was all-encompassing. Every breath Evie took was heavily laced with warm moisture. Her lungs were sure to rebel soon but she followed in silence.

Despite the chilling wails, Evie continued moving forward in the darkness. Their feet fell on stone, carved into a smooth passage by thousands of doomed feet. The walls were close on either side of them and Evie marveled at the carvings. The stone was black as the midnight sky, uneven throughout, and carved into the surface were the faces of a thousand men. Could that be a tribute of sorts to specific souls? Evie's feet slowed in their trotting to keep up with Gavriel. Her fascinated eyes remained trained on the realistic workmanships of the craft-men who had hewn such lifelike faces from rough rock.

Evie drew closer to the face of the wall. Closer to one carving, rendered at eye level. If she touched it the dull, grey skin would be leathery, hanging wrinkled from high cheekbones. As if it belonged to a man used to generous second helpings, who of a sudden was forced to starve. Skin folded at the corners of his eyes and wrinkled at his forehead, doubled below his chin. He looked in Evie's direction as if caught in the act of watching them pass.

Evie stood transfixed, staring at the carvings eyes. Both were shut while every wrinkled and pore was visible. Even the individual hairs of his eyelashes lay resting on his dull cheeks. The rendition was so life-like, Evie half expected to see the carving come to life. What skill of the carvers to create such a masterpiece here within the depths of Death.

All along the passage were thousands of similar carvings, each so different, so realistic.

Something caught Evie's eye. A movement? Light flickering on something? She looked back at the wall and at the carved face she had just inspected so closely.

And the hairs at the back of her neck lifted.

Then man stared back at her solemnly.

The whites were milky, unblemished by red blood vessels. Pitch black pupils bled like liquid smoke into the rest of the eye, threatening to overwhelm the whites. The face still looked down the passage while the eyes stared straight at Evie. She blinked, certain this was just her overactive imagination. Especially when the pair of eyes staring at her out of the stone wall held an expression of a sad combination of despair and hope.

Then he smiled.

A pathetic, gross attempt at a smile that revealed a toothless black orifice and leathery flaccid lips curled in a grin better described as a grimace. Evie stepped back in horror. The macabre face was no carving after all. This was a man, embedded within the stone wall. Evie's muscles tightened as she turned to run. A distant part of her brain registered her direction was all wrong. She was heading in the direction of the entrance while Gavriel was way ahead of her somewhere within the tunnels. At that moment it didn't matter. Sooner or later he will realize she was not in his exalted company and then he would return for her.

She may have gotten away if the hand had not grabbed her ankle. As she fell she looked down at the hand that gripped her foot. Cold, thin gnarled fingers, covered by loose, grey skin, held her ankle in it's creepy grip. Dozens and dozens of faces stared at her as she fell, hundred's of eyes observed her descent. Hundreds of hands reached for her body, desperate to grab hold of her.

Evie was equally desperate to get away, but she was caught in something of a trance. Watching the hand scratch at her body with bloody fingers. Her blood. Glistening at the tips of fingers bare of skin, where chipped nails that scraped at Evie like tiny knives, scraping at her flesh, releasing the blood as if they ached for the source of life. She began to breathe faster and harder. She was still falling. Braced herself for the impact with the stone floor, helpless to stop her journey. The hands still grasped her, fingers digging painfully into her calf.

Suddenly another pair of arms seemed to sprout from the passage floor, curving around her just as she fell. Hysterical with fear Evie scratched and scrabbled to get free from the hands despite their warmth and gentleness.

"Shh. Calm down. It is just me." Gavriel touched her arm, his cool angelic skin immediately calming. Only long enough kick out at the hand which still clung to her ankle. In one flick of a heel she dislodged the arms from both her ankle and the face on the wall. The hand went spinning across the floor, still grabbing at the air in the vain hope of clutching onto something to stop its spin. Evie stared, repulsed but transfixed as it came to a sudden stop against the opposite wall. "Did I not tell you to keep close?"

"I thought I saw something," she answered, without looking at Gavriel. Her eyes remained on the twitching hand that now reminded her of an injured spider.

"And you did." Gavriel nodded at the walls. A thousand faces carved into the walls, eyes closed and silent. Anyone would think she had imagined it all.

"Did you see it too?" Evie was desperate for Gavriel to confirm she was not crazy.

Gavriel was silent and Evie's heart plummeted. But when he answered he said, "Tartarus is filled with billions of dead. The very walls of the place are built with their bodies."

He got his feet and she rose with him until at last she was standing on two wobbly legs. Still shaken, she eyed the walls, just to make certain they were no longer alive.

"Stay close to me and as far away from the walls as possible." Gavriel started walking, the angle at which he held his head more relaxed, which Evie took as a sign that his anger was slowly dissipating .

She followed his instructions and soon they were striding along the dark passage. Evie smiled. Gavriel had saved her butt again.

The passage came to an abrupt end and had it not been for Gavriel standing firmly in front of her she would have fallen straight over the edge. The passage ended at a tiny outcropping, no balustrade, no balcony. To their right, a set of tiny stairs hugged the cliff-face and meandered downward.

Evie peered around Gavriel and gasped. Below them was a ravine where jagged spikes of rock reached skyward, beckoning for their next victim's impalement. Pale bodies were scattered around the base of the canyon, all speared through by the spikes.

And all very much alive and very much in agony.

CHAPTER 18

*E*vie averted her gaze and looked straight ahead. A deep valley expanded before her eyes, dark and foreboding. Across the valley, directly ahead of them, sat a black temple, complete with gleaming obsidian columns. From this side of the valley they could still make out the vipers coiled around the columns and writhing in a heap along the steps. Evie shuddered.

The serpent encased stairway was their destination. To their left was a winding flight of stairs hewn straight from the rock-face. It was wide enough for one person but so small that the slightest wrong step would send her plummeting to her death. Thankfully they wouldn't need to get through the jagged ravine by foot.

"We are flying right?" she asked.

"Only until we reach the edge of the rift valley. From there on we have to make it by foot," Gavriel answered, his voice low.

At Evie's frown he said, "Flying would attract attention. And attention is not what we want. Not here."

Evie nodded. Better not to say anything and get Gavriel back on edge. Since he'd saved her from those horrible questing dead hands, he had been much gentler with her. They'd spoken a few times. Yes. Definitely gentler.

They released their wings in a sudden rush of air and angel dust. The sounds of two soft implosions announced their release.

Evie sighed and Gavriel sighed with her. Both were relieved. It was always this way. As long as her wings were tucked away she felt bound, constricted as if she were holding her breath constantly. Now, with her wings stretched out behind her she could breathe at last.

Then they stepped off the edge in unison and made short work of the distance over the ravine. It didn't take long before they arrived at the last deep passageway that opened into the bared fields of the valley. In a whoosh that resembled soft thunder, Gavriel landed and quickly tucked his wings behind his back. Evie followed suit and peered around his shoulder.

"Great, another bleak dead valley, does the scenery never change here?" she asked softly. She shouldn't have bothered to ask the question because she already knew the answer.

"There is Asphodel and Elysium. But neither of those places would ever keep Daniel. Ever." He spoke with a certain satisfaction as if he was well pleased that Daniel would be denied entrance to the two places of peace and beauty within the walls of the realms of Hell.

"Once we enter the valley be sure to remain quiet. Do not talk to anyone. Try not to turn anyone's attention to you." Gavriel frowned, his face dark and serious.

"Sure thing." Evie smiled assuringly. Then she schooled her features as worry stabbed her gut. Gavriel's face was far too serious for any further banter.

They left the safety of the rock wall and walked up a barren road. The valley heaved and fell with hundreds of small hills and hillocks, divided by dozens of small streams of bubbling lava. Evie could just make out, in the distance, a gurgling stream, pulsing away from them, out of the valley.

A stream of what looked suspiciously like blood. Evie swallowed hard. A river of blood.

Barren trees dotted the valley, reminding Evie of the valley she'd first encountered on her arrival in Hades.

Their path soon brought them within sight of a group of women, dressed in ragged flowing robes, once white and pristine. Large white jars, painted with elegant gold leaf, were jammed upon shoulders or on hips. The jars were painted with joyous scenes; happy dancing maidens frolicked in meadows, and splashed in rivers, eating fruit from an abundant orchard, and playing lyres. The picture of all-round happiness.

The group of women trailed down to a thin stream whose waters sped along, clear and sparkling. The stream was so tiny, barely wide enough to place a foot and thus neither wide enough nor deep enough to fill the jars. There was only one place in the stream that allowed them to do so. A small rift in the earth had created a tiny waterfall that splashed merrily into a shallow pool below. Every so often the splashing ceased as a woman placed a jar beneath the gushing waterfall and caught the flow of the stream within its mouth.

Once filled, the woman left the river and trailed up the hill to a marble pool. The pearlescent, blue-veined marble of the pool was starkly out of place in this dark and almost evil place. As the women passed to the pool Evie stared at their faces. Each of them was a classic beauty, not just pretty but stunningly beautiful even without the artifice of makeup. But their faces were marked with unhappiness. So unlike the maidens painted on the jars they carried. Eyes were narrowed in frustration, pale skin was marred with splotches of red, dark smudges marked many an eye. They gave off an air of dejected despair which became clearer to Evie only once she and Gavriel drew abreast of the pool. They were careful to maintain their distance though.

The marble bath was a beautiful structure and would certainly have been a luxurious place to soak in cool waters. But only a few dregs of water lay on the smooth surface of the bottom of the pool. Evie was aghast. She stared again at the women and it soon became apparent that something was wrong. Their garments were heavy with water, the fabric stuck to their thighs, drenched and sopping wet from water that sloshed from the jars as they walked to the bath. She watched one woman reach the pool and tip the jar out into the bath. Only a single drop fell from the lip of the receptacle.

The jars were filled with holes and leaked their contents as the women made their way from the stream to the pool.

"What's happening?" Evie hissed softly to Gavriel who had halted beside her to watch the women.

"These are the Danaides." He stated. At her raised eyebrows he continued patiently. "The Danaides were the fifty beautiful daughters of Danuas who were all betrothed to the fifty sons of Aegyptus. The women expressed their dissatisfaction at the marriages by planning to kill their husband's on the wedding night."

"Guess they succeeded then?"

"Minos decreed they could only be absolved from their guilt if they bathed in the Waters of Absolution. That's the stream over there." Gavriel looked at the stream, and Evie turned to do the same. "The only way to be submerged in those waters is to fill the bath and soak within it. Unfortunately, Minos and the other judges failed to mention that there was one minor detail. The jugs could never be filled. So they are doomed to carry those jars between the waters and the bath, for all eternity."

"Like Sisyphus?" Evie asked.

"Exactly like him."

"Seem a bit unfair, don't you think?" Evie asked dryly.

"Maybe less so once you consider this was the premeditated murder of fifty men. All of whom were the sons of their father's brother."

"Okay, then." Evie turned to the doomed woman and sighed

softly. It was hard to watch them in their despair. Despite knowing the task was impossible, they continued, like Sisyphus, out of despair. Perhaps they still held some hope in their soul but it all seemed so pointless. Evie turned and walked ahead, unable to watch them knowing they were eternally damned.

She and Gavriel continued their journey. They walked and soon the black temple glared down at them from the cliff-top, like a black mausoleum with all knowing black eyes, watching them as they progressed up the hill.

They were not far from the step to the temple when they came upon a tree, barren of leaves, with branches as dark and scorched as soot. Impossibly, a lone fruit hung on one branch. So ripe and juicy. Evie licked her lips, She could taste the juice of the peach and could almost feel the sweet liquid run down her arms to her elbows, unheeded.

Beneath the tree, ankle deep in a pool of water, stood a large man. He stared up at the fruit, licking his parched and cracked lips, as if contemplating whether to take the peach or not. Then he reached for it, possibly hunger forcing his hand upward. The movement revealed his ribs, poking through skin so thin she could almost make out the white glare of the bones beneath. His fingers grabbed at the fruit and almost won it's prize when the branch lifted as if some mysterious hand pulled it out of his grasp.

The man sighed in frustration, reminding Evie so much of Sisyphus. Then he rose higher. In the pool, his ankles broke the surface of the pool. He raised himself onto his toes and reached further. His fingers grazed the fine white hair on the skin of the fruit, again almost grasping the peach.

Almost.

Again, cruelly, the tree pulled the fruit away and the man lowered his hand. He looked down, dejected, hopeless and still hungry. At his feet the waters churned and he licked his lips again.

CHAPTER 19

*H*e bent to cup the water in his hand but the churning waters receded and soon he stood in a small puddle of mud. Despair filled his eyes and he stared at his feet in silence. The tree groaned above and the bough lowered itself, teasing the man with its succulent fruit. The man smiled and reached for the fruit again. Evie clenched her jaw, the muscles of her fingers clenching. This wasn't right. He should know by now there was no hope. The tree was just going to pull the fruit away at the last minute and he'd be hungry again.

"So who is this sorry bastard, then?" Evie asked, anger flooding her veins. Sure this was hell but a few of the punishments she'd seen did really balance out with the crime. And made her furious.

"This poor soul is Tantalus. Doomed to forever covet the succulent fruit, to forever crave the waters at his feet to quench his thirst."

"What did he do then? Murder entire villages? Kill newborns in cold blood?" Evie asked, her voice rising in indignation.

"He made the mistake of coveting another man's wife."

"Huh? Adultery? That is reason to be internally damned to this?" Evie stabbed her finger at the scene before them, as if Gavriel had been the one who decreed Tantalus' punishment.

Gavriel smiled but covered the expression hastily. "It was not just a man's wife he coveted. And won. I might add." Gavriel replied. "When a man commits a crime against a God the punishment is a hefty one. It has consequences."

"And this is justified? Just because the woman was wife to a God?" Evie was shocked. "None of these people have committed anything worse than what humans do to each other on a daily basis. Why have I not seen a mass-murderer anywhere yet? I see a man who thought he was smarter than the King of the Gods. I see women forced to marry men they do not want and who are punished for attempting to free themselves. I see a man guilty only of falling for another man's wife, who you say he won so the woman was part of the relationship too. Guess she's not anywhere around here is she?"

By the end of her rant, Evie's voice has risen enough for Tantalus to look in their direction. In his eyes she saw the dregs of hope perhaps, although his despair won out hands down. He opened his mouth, as if to call out to them, raised his hand to hail them.

Gavriel grasped Evie's hand and pulled her down the path.

"Now see what you have done," Gavriel hissed. "Did I not tell you to try not to attract attention?"

"Why not?" These poor souls don't look like they are about to come running at us with spears and arrows," Evie bit out, refusing to accept it was entirely her own fault.

A loud cawing rang across the valley and Gavriel increased his pace. Soon they were running headlong for the ebony steps carved into the rock. Up the steps they pounded, as Evie wondered what horrible creature they ran from. A dread stabbed her in the gut, knowing she'd be to blame now for opening her big mouth.

Air surged above her and Evie's head snapped up. All she saw was a pair of enormous bird's talons. Talons that ended in nails as large as her upper body. Now, too afraid to search out the sky for their attacker, Evie ran faster then she knew she could. Stupid. If she had only listened to Gavriel in the first place, they would not be in danger of being some horrific bird's dinner.

At last, after what seemed an eternity of stairs, thigh muscles throbbing and burning, lungs on fire, they reached the entrance to the temple. The obsidian pillars lent a shadowed air to the building and spitting vipers lashed out at them in warning.

Both Gavriel and Evie ignored the hissing snakes and brushed right past them. Rather a snake bite that being slashed open by those sharp talons. The bird screeched and the pillars of the temple shook. Even the vipers fell silent. Outside, a shadow darkened the entrance to the building, and Evie stared into eyes as large as her own head. Glassy and black the bird's eye blinked at her, as if contemplating whether to bother to chase after them within the temple. Then, in a flash of feathers and a rush of air the bird turned and flew off.

Evie and Gavriel moved further into the temple, relieved to be rid of their avian pursuer. Evie dared not look at Gavriel, sure he must be angry with her again.

At the center of the temple sat a curved table, occupied by three majestic males. They looked ordinary enough, that was until Gavriel and Evie drew closer and stood a few paces from the table.

"Made it here alive did you?" The man on the right said. His skin was pale, his hair a shock of white that Einstein would have been proud of. His dark eyes studied the visitors, a contemplative look on his face.

Gavriel inclined his head respectfully. "We had a few problems along the way."

"I hope you have not disturbed our .... inmates." He smiled and turned to Evie. "Ah! So this is the reason you are here, Gavriel?"

Evie threw a questioning glance in Gavriel's direction but he just looked at the man who spoke. Perhaps his actions meant it was safer to be polite.

"Yes. I am here to see Daniel."

All three men frowned in disapproval but said nothing.

"Evangeline has the right to speak to her father."

"Not if her father has no rights."

Evie suppressed a sigh. Even she could not have said it better.

There was a painful silence, during which Evie bit her tongue to ensure she did not launch into a tirade of pleading.

"She wishes to speak with him one last time." Gavriel spoke quietly. "That is why we have come. We respectfully request your consideration." The archangel bowed his head and waited.

"Come now, enough of this obeisance nonsense, Archangel. What we need to know is why we should allow this."

"For a thousand years I have tracked my father's movements, learned his history, admired and respected him. All that time I was desperate to find him, have him look at me and be proud that he had a daughter who lived in his light." The men stared at Evie in silence. She paused for breath, hadn't realized she was holding it in the first place. "Until I found out who my real father was, I felt I was someone special. Now I am not so sure anymore."

"But what would you gain from speaking to him now, my dear?" The man in the middle asked her as he shook his head, his gray hair wispy and soft around his head. His voice was gentle although his grey eyes gleamed strong and gave Evie the impression he could see right into her soul.

"I just need him to know. And I need to know why he abandoned me." Evie glanced over at Gavriel. Silent permission to continue. "And I need to know how he could have allowed the Control to kill my mother. How he could have allowed anyone to kill his own child. I just need ..." She stopped speaking mainly because she was incredibly afraid she would begin to cry and the last thing she needed now was to shed tears. She needed to appear strong, in control of her faculties. Would these men allow a wailing imbecile to enter the dungeons of Tartarus?

"Closure." The last man, who had been silent all along, spoke in a voice that had an almost musical ring to it. His face was craggy, and handsome, his brows as dark as his shoulder-length hair.

Evie nodded, relieved that at least one of the men before her understood her deep need to see Daniel.

The three men looked at each other and Gavriel walked over to the table, handing them a scroll. Evie's eyes widened. She hadn't seen the scroll before. Where had he hidden it all this time? Evie snorted silently at her presumption. Of course, archangel glamor is strong enough to be impervious even to a Nephilim.

Gavriel walked to her side and grasped her hand. He drew her away from the table.

"They will confer and tell us the verdict," he said, his eyes still on the three men and the scroll.

"What was that you just gave them?"

"Julian's recommendation," Gavriel said, the words sounding clipped and almost angry again. Evie bit her lip, forcing her mouth to remain shut. Julian had sent a recommendation to the judges in spite of thinking this whole thing was stupid and dangerous. Heat rushed her, followed strongly by a rush of emotion. Julian was actually supporting her in this even though he'd behaved as if he wasn't. What did it mean? Evie flushed warm all over with the realization that Julian was helping her because he cared. The same reason Gavriel was helping her. They'd both been so angry with her, and in the face of that anger Evie had been angry right back.

Angry and insolent. But all this time they just wanted to protect her. As if she didn't know she was very aware that Daniel would reject her. She expected nothing less from him. And she cared nothing for his affections. It was his answer to those two questions that she wanted.

Why did you let them kill my mother and why did you let them take me?

CHAPTER 20

*W*hile they waited for the verdict Evie observed the three men.

They were nodding among themselves. The Judge on the right spoke softly, a worried scowl creasing his face. He shook his head, his white hair floating around him like a soft cloud.

"Who is he?" Evie asked softly, deciding it was high time she knew the names of these Judges who held her fate in their hands.

"He is Minos of Crete," Gavriel said. "The one in the middle is Aeacus, once King of Aegina. On the right is Rhadamantus. They are brothers, all human sons of Zeus.""

"They were human? Not Gods then?"

"No, not Gods. Their actions in life proved they would be good, impartial judges."

Evie wanted to snort out loud. *Impartial judges my ass.* How impartial was tricking the Danaides into believing they would attain absolution. What was fair about that?

"Best if you don't voice those thoughts," Gavriel said softly.

"Are you reading my mind?" she asked.

"No, your face tells me exactly what you are thinking and

voicing those thoughts here and now will get you in a whole heap of trouble. And perhaps end your plea to see Daniel," he said, keeping his gaze trained on the three judges still deliberating.

"Anyone thinking Nepotism here?" Evie asked after a few moments more of observing the men.

Gavriel smiled. "More than you may think. Guess being half God has its advantages."

"Mmh. Hercules and Theseus may have something to say about that," Evie responded, not too sure how she felt about the rules and regulations of the Underworld. Julian, within his cave palace seemed so unlike his kingdom. Perhaps, having taken over an already established Kingdom, Julian had little to say on its structure and law. He was just the curator until His Highness figured out where he had lost himself in the first place.

A rumble rose from the table as the three Judges seemed to disagree on the terms of Evie's permissions. She sighed.

Nothing is ever easy is it?

Aeacus spoke in his low thundering voice, "Come forth, Archangel and bring the Nephilim with you. We have decided."

Although Evie bristled at the 'Nephilim' reference she followed him. They moved slowly and stood before the table. Evie's heart hovered somewhere below her ribs. This was it.

"We have decided to allow the Nephilim to visit the Archangel prisoner," Minos spoke and Evie tensed, not sure if elation was the correct response but feeling the rise in her heartbeat anyway. And then her heart plummeted as she saw the narrowing of Minos' green eyes. "There are some conditions though."

Naturally there were conditions. Evie felt Gavriel tense beside her, but he remained silent. It should have been obvious from the eternal punishments of Sisyphus and Tantalus, and even the Danaides that the justice of the Gods of the Underworld was never straight or just. She had known, had suspected something like this might happen but all the same she was intensely disappointed.

Gavriel and Evie waited in silence to hear the stipulations.

"We have a task, collateral and two boons." Minos smiled as if he had bestowed her with the gift of Aphrodite's beauty. Instead it felt like a nest of vipers, sisters to the ones coiled and hissing at the entrance to this black temple. Minos continued. Clearly they were not expected to ask any questions. "The task is simple. We wish you to retrieve the Pearl of Kampe."

This time Gavriel stiffened and did not keep silent. "But that is almost impossible. Evangeline is no match for Kampe." Gavriel looked at Evie, a silent once-over as if to confirm for himself that what he claimed was true. "Neither of us are any sort of match for a Drakaene."

Evie had read somewhere that Kampe was a half-dragon, half-woman, serpent monster. She shuddered to think what a weak chance she might have against a powerful creature like that, who could snap a man in two with her bare hands. And then devour him just to be sure he was dead.

"That is where the collateral comes in." Minos smiled. For a King who was renowned for his goodness and charity, the sly curve to his smile was confirmation enough that he was enjoying the stakes of the game.

Aeacus rose and pointed one finger at Gavriel, as if in accusation. Evie did not expect the bolt of pure light that sparked from the Judge's finger. It struck the angel, then merely circled around Gavriel in an flickering embrace. At once, Gavriel was encased up to his shoulders within a black marble pillar. It would have held most people but the Judge had forgotten they were dealing with God's Archangel. Not some puny human. The marble shook as if an eruption was building up within the column, and before Evie could exhale Gavriel burst from the column in a shower of black stones and dust.

It appeared that she had misjudged the God-men who sat before her. Minos rose and from his side he drew a gleaming silver-white object shaped like a lightning bolt. Heavy artillery.

He pointed the bolt at Gavriel, aimed and let loose a thunderbolt so loud the building shook and the snakes hissed in unison.

Gavriel had no chance. None at all.

Shocked and horrified, Evie stared at Gavriel, or rather, what he had become. The bolt had not disintegrated the Archangel as she had expected to. No, it had in fact cast the living Gavriel into a solid statue. A strange glow radiated from him. From his skin and face and body. She was sure the shimmer had nothing to do with the Angelic nature of the prisoner. Perhaps it was whatever power emanated from the bolt that now entranced Gavriel into an un-moving solid statue.

Great.

How was that for helping her out? Immediately Evie had the grace to be ashamed of her ungratefulness and her ingratitude. Gavriel had brought her all the way only because she'd wanted to come. No matter how much he disagreed with her, he supported her all the way. What in Hades was she supposed to do with Kampe in Gavriel's absence?

She steeled her voice and twisted her fingers around each other to stop the shaking. "If that is the collateral what are the boons?"

"The boons are what you came here for. You wanted to speak to Daniel? So you shall. Gavriel here shall have the chance to see his wife in Elysium." Almost as an afterthought he said. "And there shall be a boon for you which ... well let me just say you will know it when you receive it."

Evie shivered.

But it was not fear which rippled through her body and coursed through her very flesh. It was pure violent anger at being duped. She was about to say just that when she caught Gavriel's eye. His entire body was petrified. All except his eyes. The skin and flesh below his right eye were frozen much like the rest of him, pulling his face into a grotesque, almost unrecognizable shape. But Gavriel still managed to stare straight into her soul.

His voice echoed in her mind, like a spirit lost.

Don't say a word. This is all you are going to get. Take it. And be careful.

CHAPTER 21

*E*vie stood outside the temple feeling bereft and alone. Part of her was glad she left the judgment hall. Seeing Gavriel solidified in the pillar was unbearable enough without the terrible knowledge that his life, and probably hers too, now lay in the success or failure of her task.

Kampe.

What did she know about Kampe? She was a half-woman, half-dragon who could probably eat Evie alive just for looking at her. And Minos thought Evie was capable of finding this Pearl, whatever it was? He was sending her on a mission to retrieve jewels. She stopped herself from shaking her head in disgust.

But just maybe he knew she was not capable, knew she would fail. And when she failed he would have Gavriel and Evie both stuck down here in Tartarus for as long as he pleased. She wouldn't put it past him either. She didn't trust any of these Judges. Not with their track records. Evie suspected the three Judges had an ulterior motive for the task. It seemed as if they had been well prepared for her request. Whatever it was they were after, Evie could only wonder.

Her feet were now planted on the first step of the marble

temple. They felt like lead weights. Like the rest of her body. It was impossible. She stared out at the black valley, her heart heavy in her breast. Impossible. She had no idea where to go. Gavriel was incapable of telling her. She hesitated and glanced over her shoulder, peering into the darkness of the black temple. Perhaps the Judges would give her some direction?

But, when she returned to the Hall, all that remained was the stone Gavriel. She stood there for a long and silent moment, studying the angel. When Minos had struck him with the bolt Evie had thought he'd transformed Gavriel into a solid form of himself. On closer inspection she realized she'd been wrong. The angel was encased in a clear tube of nothing, as if embedded within a pillar of glass, unable to move, unable to help her.

Angry, and frustrated, Evie hit the column with the flat of her hand, the sharp crack of skin hitting solid glass rang through the Hall, mocking her from the carved cornices, and the engraved pillars encircling the Hall.

Gavriel stared back at her. Shared frustration simmered between them.

"Help me," Evie cried. Then considered how incongruous her words were. She straightened. She was not the one encased in a pillar of glass. She, at least, was able to walk around, breathe, talk.

She lay her heated forehead against the calming coolness of the pillar.

Well, at least it's good for something, she thought, angry with herself and the Judges.

At last she raised her head, to say goodbye to Gavriel. She had to leave. Be on her way to find Kampe. Gavriel met her eyes and within them she found not an ounce of hopelessness. Just strength and encouragement. As if this test was just routine.

He held her eyes, steady, then looked directly at where the Judges had sat.

Evie followed his gaze and found nothing. The marble table and chairs were gone. Not a speck dust out of place to indicate they had even been there in the first place. Evie threw a questioning glance at Gavriel to find him staring at the Hall again but this time he raised his eyes a bit. Assuming he meant to look past the Hall, Evie trained her eyes at the furthest end of the temple and noticed something marring the solid blackness of the marble. Her feet took her there of their own accord and she bent to pick up a gleaming black feather. Larger than an angel's feather, shimmering with all the colors of the rainbow, it sparkled against the dark marble. Evie stared at it as if it would soon tell her where it came from.

She shook her head in disgust. The feather was about as much help as Gavriel was. Evie opened her mouth and was about to ask the voiceless Gavriel *what now* when a screeching caw reached her ears.

The demonic bird which had chased them from Tantalus to the temple.

"That's the plan?" She looked at Gavriel. "You want me to enlist the help of a giant scavenger that just a few minutes ago wanted to have me as a snack?"

The look in Gavriel's eyes said that if he were able, he would be shaking his head, fed-up with Evie. He almost rolled his eyes and Evie felt a spurt of laughter rise in her throat.

"Okay, okay. I take the hint. I'll find the bird. Don't go anywhere okay. I'll be back." Evie spoke the words over her shoulder as she walked back to the entrance to look for the flying monstrosity with claws larger than her head.

She scanned the sky and didn't need to wait long. The avian monster swooped past, screeching at Evie like a mother scolding her young, sending a dusty, musty odor up her nostrils.

Despite her instinct saying this was most probably the stupidest thing she had done in a long time, Evie walked to the edge of the cliff. The drop to the valley below was sheer and deadly, and normally heights did not affect her, but today her stomach heaved at the sight.

"Show me where Kampe is," Evie shouted out as loud as she could, certain that Tantalus and the poor water-bearing women would hear her too.

The bird circled above Evie, as if it had heard and understood nothing. Evie sighed.

Well it was worth a try.

And she had taken Gavriel's advice so he wouldn't be able to point a finger at her for resisting his advice. She sighed and watched the bird make a wide circle above her head, then head off down the valley toward a pass up ahead.

There she goes. Probably has something better to do anyway.

Evie was about to return to Gavriel with the news of her lack of success when the creature banked wide left before making a full turn and flying back toward her. Its great black wings sent a draught of hot air toward her. It circled above her again and flew off in the direction of the pass. Once more, and Evie was certain the bird showing her the way.

Evie descended the stairs, keeping an eye on the large, dark splotch in the grey sky. It circled above as if to be sure Evie was following. Reaching the valley floor, Evie kept her eyes on the bird. Strange creature. Its wings glimmered as it flew, as if its dark feathers hid something beneath it. Something extraordinary.

Following the bird on foot became increasingly tedious and Evie decided that flight would be much more speedy and enjoyable too. A niggle of doubt irritated her, her inner voice reminding her that she shouldn't attract too much attention. In spite of her doubt, she breathed deep and centered her energy on her back, focusing dense pressure on the seam which encased her wings. Her back bulged with an answering pressure, but that was all. Evie tried again and nothing. Frustrated she tried one more time, then resumed walking, a dark scowl painting her face. Disgusted she cursed the Judges.

Another one of the tricks of the Gods of Judgment. Something they had conveniently omitted to tell her. Evie wasn't surprised. Those guys didn't seem to be the most honest of types. Evie gritted her teeth. Neither she nor Gavriel had come before the Gods to be Judged. What right did they have to pronounce a judgment and a task upon her?

Julian.

His scroll had been crucial to Evie gaining access to Tartarus, even if it meant she had to perform this task. She wondered if he would have had any power over these three Stooges to relieve her of this task?

Now forced to walk, Evie undertook that task with bad form. How long she was able to stay angry would depend on what progress she made in her task. Heading to the pass she craned her neck to see the tops of the two walls of rock as they rose and almost touched at their closest points.

She passed through the natural gateway, feeling insignificant and tiny. A mere speck of life in this dark dead place. Even the light of an angel is nothing within Tartarus and now she couldn't even use her wings.

CHAPTER 22

*T*he change in the landscape was confounding.

Passing through the gateway Evie moved into another world. Lava had flowed in rivers within this valley. Evie stood at the edge of a deep ravine dotted with columns of stone which provided a pathway to the other side. Evie's knees quivered when she looked down into the depths of the slash in the earth. A river of boiling lava flowed slow and steady within the chasm. It seemed the rise and fall of the burning river had eaten away at the rock pillars to such an extent that some of the pillars balanced on rock columns the thickness of Evie's hand.

She decided it was best to avoid those particular columns.

Still, the rocks gave Evie cold sweats, even in this sauna of a place. The bird still circled above, cawing as if asking what the delay was. Evie hesitated. With her wings bound by the stooges she had no way of saving herself should she fall from one of those columns.

The bird cawed again. Gavriel. Julian. Even Daniel. Reasons for Evie to steel herself and move ahead. She had to get the Pearl and free Gavriel. The only other option was to make herself comfortable here in Tartarus, as without the Pearl there was no way out. Even her visit with Daniel took a back seat when it came to Gavriel's life.

Evie stepped out onto the nearest stone pillar. Her knees shook and she knew that was not a good idea. She had to keep it together. There was the sense of each stone step as a floating table, so fragile, with the river of molten rock moving far below. Evie stepped onto the next stone, her heart shattering as the edge of the platform burst into a shower of shale and fell away into the red river below. She took a deep breath and focused on the next stone, stepping onto it and moving her balance as gracefully as possible. Progress was interminably slow.

Each stone seemed further and further apart until Evie found she was halfway across. Her heart thudded. The next stone step was further away, so far that Evie had to do more than lunge to make it safely onto the flat surface. She'd need a running jump to launch herself across the gaping maw of the ravine. But she didn't have sufficient space to take the leap. And without her wings she had no way to add to her anti-gravitational abilities.

Half-way there. But how to go forward without breaking her sorry neck. Evie glanced over her shoulder. But she knew that Minos was not above supplying her with any sort of temptation to force her to stray from her task. The stone path was challenge enough. Evie faced forward and eyed the next step. It was all or nothing. Looking behind her she moved to the very edge of the step then held her heart in her hand as the heel of her boot slipped. Stone shattered, spitting from beneath her foot and sending shivers of horror through Evie's body. She tamped down her hysteria even as it rose to break through her throat. She steadied herself, took a good look at the column beneath the pillar to ensure it would not break in two beneath her weight. Good.

It looked solid.

Evie took a deep breath and ran. Pushing hard, knowing she didn't have enough of a running start to take her time. At the edge she pushed off, flailing her arms hoping by some miracle it may increase the airflow beneath her. But something was wrong. There was a warm downdraft that seemed to pull on her weight and Evie felt herself begin to fall. In spite of the pull, she still persisted, aiming for the stone.

But she was falling. Perhaps to her death.

Fried angel.

Falling.

Behind her shocked lids she saw Patrick in the monastery garden grabbing hold of her ankles the first time she flew. The first time she threw a coin into the Trevie fountain in 200 AD. Patrick arguing with her for tending to the injured on the battlefields of the Holy War, risking her life because she was not immune to death. Isabella, the beautiful little girl she'd played with who grew to be a ruthless Queen. Ling, who mouthed off at Evie the first time they met. Ash's incomparable beauty that was sometimes blinding. Even Flash and his quirky smile.

Then her fingers caught at the edge of the step, heat bursting over her fingertips where her nails ripped off as she grabbed the edge of stone. She held on, her heart thudding, everything now hinging on whether she was able to get herself back up again. Without shattering the stone.

It seemed impossible now.

Her feet dangled in the air above the roiling lava. Her useless wings pressing against her back, wanting out. Evie hated herself for relying on her wings so much. But her training had not been for nothing. All that sword-fighting shooting with her bow had strengthened her upper arms. Slowly she put all her strength into her upper arms, using her muscles to pull herself up on her fingers, high enough to hook an elbow and a knee over the edge.

For one fearful second Evie's head swam. Fear. Vertigo. It didn't really matter. All that mattered was that if she gave in it could well mean the death of her. So she grabbed on harder. A knee found purchase, then a thigh. She hung butt down until she got her breath then lifted herself over the edge and collapsed dead center of the step. She'd be hyperventilating soon if she weren't careful, but she lay still and tried to think of something happy. But all she could see was Gavriel's stony face and staring eyes.

The bird cawed and brought her back to reality.

Back to the realization that she lay shivering upon a column of stone which could potentially collapse into the molten river below. Evie roused herself, pushing through the lethargy of shock which gripped her, clouding her vision.

Slowly Evie got to her feet, pushing up through the quivering in her knees. Thankfully the next two steps were easy enough to maneuver, just two small leaps which were fairly stress-free. Not so easy when one's knees were wobbly, but she made it. When she reached the last one her heart fell.

The other side was too far away. Too far to jump. She peered over the edge. The ragged remnants of another stone step lay between her. The last step before freedom. If she jumped and missed she would be skewered like a piece of meat, with jagged pieces of rock piercing through her body.

The breath that left her was somewhere between a sigh and a wail. Now what? Going back was not an option. Going forward seemed impossible. This was beginning to be too much effort. Why did she ever say she wanted to see Daniel? If she had known there was this much effort involved she would easily have just dealt with her awful murderous parent by forgetting him.

She certainly hadn't had it in mind to be risking her very life for him. She sighed and reminded herself of Gavriel, stuck in his glass column prison. Of his eyes staring out at her unable to express what he wanted her to know. Of the possibility he could see his wife in Elysium. It was now for Gavriel that she risked her life. A part of Evie no longer cared if she ever got to see Daniel. But for Gavriel she could not give up. Thankfully she had understood what he meant about the bird.

The bird.

Evie scanned the skies, craning her head to find the damned creature. The skies were a constant drab grey, dull as ever. Stood to reason since no sun shone in the underworld.

She squinted. There it was, flying a tight circle, high above her. So high it was a mere speck of dust in her vision. Evie waved, then figured waving wasn't going to get the birds attention, so she put two fingers into her mouth and let out an ear-splitting whistle. Long and loud enough that the bird would hear.

It worked. The speck became a blob, and soon transformed into a noticeable bird shape. It didn't take long for the creature to be close enough that Evie could see the striations of rainbow colors glistening in the oily blackness of the feathers. The bird flew past her, buffeting Evie with a gust of air.

"Help me," she yelled. Then she laughed at herself, shaking her head as tears filmed her eyes. She was actually talking to a giant bird.

She looked up and gritted her teeth in frustration. The creature had no idea what she wanted it to do. It tired of flying past her in long sweeps and drew away from her. Then it turned, swooping back down on her like an eagle aiming its deadly talons at its prey.

When she saw the claws, glistening in the weak grey light she panicked. She spared a moment to snort, appreciating the irony. She was stuck between a claw and a hot place. A really hot place. This was it then. She shut her eyes, clenched her body for the impact. For the giant claws to rip into her flesh and spear her.

Evie opened her eyes when she felt herself become weightless. She was floating, almost flying. Where moments ago there was solid stone beneath her feet, now there was nothing. She felt a sharp tension beneath her arms and glanced behind her. The huge claws were fastened beneath her arms, lifting her across the last impossible step toward the solid ground across from her. It had understood what she wanted. She didn't want to even try and understand how the creature had known what she needed. Maybe the same way the bird had known she needed its guidance to get to Kampe, but Evie wasn't going to waste time trying to figure it out.

It let her down slow enough for Evie to get her footing, releasing her just in time for her to make a running landing. The bird swooped around her and landed beside her in a flurry of wings and black dust just as she skidded to a stop.

It stood before Evie, its black head cocked to the side, one glassy eye staring at her, almost contemplative.

"Thank you." Evie felt slightly embarrassed talking to a bird of all things. But there was something strange in the way the creature was staring at her. It wasn't as if it could answer her anyway.

"Do not thank me, angel." The voice surrounded Evie like the arms of a loved one, caressing and warm. Evie spun around, but there was nobody behind her. Turning back to the bird she almost fell over her own feet. It said a lot about her mental state when her dexterity was this pathetic.

The bird was gone.

CHAPTER 23

*I*n its place stood a tall woman. Her pale skin glowed with a luminescence that could not be attributed to the dull grey light of the fake sky above. Her long blonde hair flowed over her shoulder and her robes gleamed white and silken.

"Who are you?" Evie shivered in the face of the eerie pale beauty of this woman. Woman? No, this was no woman.

"I am Hecate." She smiled and moved closer to Evie, until she was but inches from her face. Evie wasn't sure if she should move, wasn't sure if she like the perusal as Hecate walked slowly around her, as if examining a slave for the bargaining.

Evie swallowed, and found her throat dry. "Why did you help me?" This was important as one thing Evie knew was Gods never did anything for Humans unless they gained in some way.

Right on cue Hecate said, "I have my reasons. Come, I will show you the way." The goddess turned, pale and mysterious. Evie followed in silence, not daring to ask further questions. They walked along a ridge of rocks that towered so high above that they seemed to lean inward and threatened to crash to the ground at the slightest movement. A maze of rocky outcroppings, crevices and caves.

Soon Hecate drew to a stop and turned. Evie would never have found this cave without her help. A jab of dislike hit her, twisting deep within her gut. Another of the Stooges neat little tricks to ensure Evie failed. What would they have to gain from her failure?

Evie stared at Hecate, unsure again of what she should be saying. Having to thank a god for her help was a new experience. One which would have been better had it never happened at all. But seeing that it did, Evie wondered if she should thank Hecate again.

She never got the chance. While she deliberated her thanks, Hecate smiled and flew upward becoming the bird in half a blink of Evie's eye. She watched as Hecate circled, watching from above. This time she didn't caw.

Smart bird. Woman. Goddess.

Perhaps it was best not to warn the inhabitant of the cave.

The dark mouth beckoned, and Evie entered slowly, keeping to the walls as the passage wound down and around a large cavernous room. If this was Kampe's home, then Kampe needed to call in a cleaning service.

Soon.

Evie tucked herself within the shadows and listened. Water trickled somewhere in the cave. A cat mewled from a far corner. Flames flickered in a stray draught. Something was dragged across the floor of the cave, slithering, slippery and scaly in unison. And breathing. She reached for her weapons, knife and sword comfortable in each hand, and moved forward step by step.

The room was empty except for little mewling sounds that echoed around and around, disorienting Evie. She shook her head and concentrated, trying hard to pick out the direction of the crying. She moved toward the sound, cautious, aware that

Kampe may return at any minute. In the corner, on a bed of linen, Evie found the source of the mewling. Not a cat, but a baby.

A beautiful infant.

That was when she felt the air move behind her. Too late to react, the blow hit her like a sledge-hammer and Evie went tumbling across the floor, sending baskets of fabrics and other unknown objects skittering in all directions.

Evie tried to get to her feet as quickly as possible but her head was spinning, she couldn't even think straight let alone rise to her feet.

"Who are you?" the voice hissed, loud as if right in her ear. Looking for the voice at her side, Evie found the face of a woman who had once been a great beauty. Now ravaged by age and hatred and death, only the last vestiges of beauty remained. And those remnants were tossed to the wind as Evie's eyes followed the line of the woman's body. Her torso was female, with pendulous breasts, her body skeletal, covered by long, matted hair. From the waist her body split in two, as if each of her legs were a different living creature. On the left a snakes body coiled ending in a rattling tip just inches from Evie's foot. The other was a scorpions tail, gleaming black with a stinger that looked more deadly than a real scorpion's tail.

The legs were shocking enough but the belt closed the deal. Encircling her waist were the heads of dozens of wild animals. Bears, tigers, lions, hyenas, jackals, panthers. Every kind of carnivorous creature and more than Evie had never even seen before.

Evie scrambled backward until her back met cold stone. Nowhere to go. And Kampe just advanced on her.

Evie could do nothing but wait for her fate.

"Speak." Kampe's scorpion tail waved over Evie's head and closed the distance to the soft flesh of Evie's cheek. The cold, dark point of the stinger traced a line down her cheek and the

Evie sat paralyzed with fear. This was not what was supposed to happen. Where the hell was this pearl anyway? Kampe's neck and hands were bare of any adornment. The cave was a hovel and even if she kept a pearl hidden here, how would Evie ever know where to look.

The stinger traced its way under Evie's chin and pressed against the soft skin, forcing Evie to rise to her feet to avoid being impaled on the sharp point. Kampe's eyes glittered, venom swirling in the whites. Perhaps it was time she spoke. Before she had a nasty meeting with the business end of Kampe's scorpion limb.

"I'm looking for someone." Evie searched desperately for a name. Any thing to satisfy Kampe.

"Tell me who, girl, and I may spare your life." The voice rippled along Evie's skin, raising goose bumps all across her arms.

"My mother." Evie saw the hand of the baby reach into the air above her, a tiny foot raised to touch the toe. Pink flesh so pure and pearly white. Pearly. The realization slammed into Evie, stunning her.

The Pearl of Kampe.

The baby was the Pearl. She had to steal Kampe's baby from her.

"Who is your mother?" The words were hissed into her ear as Kampe turned and sent a tender glance at the infant.

"I don't know. All I know is that my father allowed her to be killed and I have come to find her." Evie hoped the monster would not take the time to think through her lie. Besides, she had no intention of sticking around long enough.

With Kampe's attention fixed on the infant, Evie ducked beneath the stinger, sliding her dagger back into her boot. She would have better range with the sword and she needed a free hand for the baby. She ran around the cave crouching low as she scrambled to the child. As soon as Evie fled, Kampe caught sight of her and screamed her rage. The babe screamed with her, fearful now of the awful sound filling the cave. Evie's ears hurt so badly that she was slightly disoriented, a little off balance. But she pinned her eye on the baby and ran.

One round around the cavern got her to the child. Kampe, concentrating on Evie, had no idea of the angel's intention or she would have been protecting her baby.

Evie bent low, raced passed the basket that held the child. As she flew past she hooked her free arm through the handles. She kept running, keeping an eye out for Kampe.

That was a mistake.

The creature was incomparably large, both her limbs having great range. As Evie headed for the rising path up to the entrance, she heard the screaming she-dragon behind her. Evie refused to look back, afraid of what she would see. She just ran. Evie reached the entrance and only then allowed herself to glance back to make sure she had a head start.

Another mistake.

Evie felt the pain before she realized the stinger had penetrated her thigh. Pain did one of two things to Evie depending on its reason and its location. Emotional pain brought tears when it was relevant. Physical pain just plain pissed her off.

Evie struck with her sword, slicing straight through the black shell of the tail, and continued running out of the cave. She ignored the stinger still embedded within her thigh.

A caw emanated from above. Hecate. Evie didn't need to bother to search the skies. She felt the air above her change, the talons curl around the straps of her backpack as she was lifted through the air.

Evie just concentrated on keeping hold of the baby.

CHAPTER 24

*I*n mid-flight there was nothing else to do but stare at the child. What did this baby have that the Judges wanted? And what would happen to Gavriel if she didn't hand the child over? So many questions. Evie didn't want to be responsible for the life of another person. The heavy flap of Hecate wings blew gusts of wind against Evie's face.

No it had nothing to do with her, this political game of the underworld. Minos and his partners, Hecate and now the Pearl. There was more going on here than Evie cared to know about.

It didn't take long for Evie's feet to touch the ground and Hecate deposited her at the base of the mountain, right in front of the stairs to the Temple of Judgment. Evie opened her mouth to thank the goddess but she ended up closing her gaping mouth as she watched Hecate rise into the air and wondered if she would ever be able to thank the Goddess properly.

Her mind full of questions, Evie trudged up the stairs with her bundle of silent baby. It was as if the child could tell that something monumental was about to happen. At the entrance to the Temple even the vipers were silent, swaying and coiling but silent. They too knew something was happening. Or maybe they were shocked that Evie had returned alive and with the prize requested by the Judges. Evie hurried forward and drew close to Gavriel and met his eyes. He still stood, imprisoned in the column. It was possible his expression was one of relief. But she couldn't be certain. A sound drew her attention to the Judgment Table, where the three Judges now sat, waiting.

Expectation was not one of the expressions on their faces. Annoyance, surprise, amusement, and a little anger perhaps. As Evie suspected most of it was almost a game to them.

"Come forward, Nephilim."

Evie stood before the table, hugging the child to her.

"I see you have the pearl." Minos leaned forward as if he expected Evie to pass the baby to him.

But she was not ready. She was at least owed an explanation. She drew the bundle away and asked, "What do you want with the child?"

"That is not your concern. Be thankful you are not expected to dispatch of Kampe's spawn as part of your task, Nephilim. Now hand over the child and you will have the archangel back, and your boons of course."

Torn, Evie looked over her shoulder. Already the glass column seemed to be melting. Her duty was to Gavriel and getting him out alive. Reluctantly, and with a heavy heart, she handed the child to Minos.

"What will you do?" Evie still wanted to know what would happen to the child.

"Why, the child as you call it, must die, of course," said Radhamantus as he pulled the swaddling off the child.

Evie stepped away from the table in shock. Pure white horror rippled through her. The child was a child no longer. Although the face still resembled a baby, the rest of the body was that of a scorpion. One which Evie had hugged so close to her chest just moments ago.

"Sometimes it is better not to believe what you see," Aeacus said quietly. With those words the judges, table and all, disappeared.

Gavriel grunted beside Evie. She grabbed for him as he crumpled to the marble floor.

"Are you okay?" she asked, panicked and still off balance, the image of the little white scorpion baby burned into her retinas.

"Yes. I'm fine. But you are not."

It seemed that all it took was for Gavriel to mention her injury for Evie to feel the pain. White hot agony ripped through her thigh and she stumbled to the ground.

The stinger.

She'd forgotten all about it. She had to get it out of her flesh. Not to prevent any further poison from leaching into her bloodstream, rather to be rid of any part of Kampe that was still with her. She shivered with disgust.

Gavriel held her up and spoke softly, "Come, we have to leave. They have kept their word but who knows how long they will hold open the door." Gavriel drew Evie to her feet and helped her toward the other side of the room. An archway had opened, beyond which stood green fields and trees laden with pure white flowers. "Someone will help us there."

Evie heard the note of hope in his voice and could not deny him that. So she kept silent and let him lead her through the doorway.

IT TURNED out to be a doorway into another world.

Elysium. Heaven in the Underworld.

Evie and Gavriel shielded their eyes against the bright glare of the white marble temple. Startling contrast to the black, viper-ridden temple of Tartarus. Green rolling meadows peeked at them through a rotunda-like circling of columns. Neither spoke as they stared at lush valleys, trees hanging heavy with fruit ripe for the picking. Their feet touched sun-warmed marble floors. Warm from the sunlight streaming through ivory marble columns.

Sunlight.

Evie ran to the steps of the Temple and stared at the sky. Some kind of miracle was happening here to create the fluffiest of cotton-wool clouds and a sky so blue it surely was above-ground. The air was cool and fresh, tinged with the crisp odor of leaves, grass and the gentle perfume of flowers. More than a pleasant change from the depths of Tartarus.

But the view would have to wait. As soon as Evie put weight on her foot, searing agony gripped her, rippling through her muscles and drawing nausea through her belly. Stars danced in front of her eyes and there was only the barest chance to take a breath.

How much of Kampe's poison already ran through her veins? Her thigh throbbed to the beat of her heart and Evie felt herself lose consciousness.

IT WAS A MERCIFUL THING, passing out. Despite being outwardly disgusted with herself for such un-warrior like behavior, Evie studied the ebony stinger as it lay on the small table beside the bed. She was secretly grateful for the bliss of unconsciousness that had saved her from the agony of its removal. Even detached from Kampe's body, it still bore a residue of evil within it. Evie still had trouble focusing. The poison had infiltrated her blood-stream so thoroughly that all that got her out of Tartarus while still standing was pure adrenalin.

Shadows shifted and a woman walked into the rotunda, gliding in on silent feet. She sat beside Evie on the bed, taking care not to disturb her. Warm hands checked the bandages wrapped around her thigh and Evie tried hard not to flinch at the inspection. The gentle smile on the woman's face reminded Evie that she had no idea who this angel of mercy was.

"Evangeline. It's about time you woke up." Gavriel entered and stood beside the woman.

It was the way their bodies touched, the barest of movements, that piqued Evie's interest. That was the action of a domesticated pair or at least two people who knew each other very, very well. Evie met Gavriel's eyes and raised one eyebrow. His returning smile was a mixture of sheepish boyishness and pride.

Placing an arm around the woman's shoulders he said, "Evie, this is Dania. My wife."

Somehow it did not surprise her at all. That the Judges would deem this as a suitable boon. That Gavriel would be this happy to be with his wife again. His wife? Evie blinked. Was there not a child included in this equation? She looked around Gavriel, hoping to see his daughter hiding behind him. Evie wanted to ask where the little girl was but Gavriel gave a tiny shake of his head and she bit her tongue. She would find out soon enough.

Then she thought of Patrick. She glanced up at Gavriel. "Is Patrick here?"

When he shook his head Evie's heart twisted. "He wouldn't be able to enter Elysium. Only those pure of soul gain access. And Patrick, with his long life and the many things he'd had to do in his lifetime, was not pure of soul."

Evie wanted to argue with that pronouncement. But she knew it would be useless. Patrick wasn't in Elysium and Evie wouldn't be able to see him. That was all there was to it. She didn't have the strength to demand more.

Instead she changed the topic. "So how do I get to see Daniel from here?" she asked gruffly, wanting everything to go back to business. Not wanting to see that sliver of pain which had glittered in Gavriel's eye for a split second. Not wanting to think about what it meant.

"Well, as soon as you are up to it, we will get it arranged."

Dania's voice was soft and gentle. Too gentle for Evie. All she wanted was to get out of there. Away from all the niceness that surely hid a black grief.

"I am fine. Can we go as soon as possible?" Evie asked Gavriel and smiled at Dania, as she rose to her feet. She didn't hear Gavriel's answer. Perhaps it was agreement. More likely it was stern admonition.

She fell heavily and was lucky to be caught by Gavriel before she hit the ground hard. Gavriel gave her an admonishing glare. There was nothing she could say to the fact that her stupid leg could not hold her weight.

She'd have to stay put for a little while until it healed.

But as soon as she was strong enough to stand she would insisted Gavriel take her to Tartarus. She didn't have any time to waste lounging around in a sick bed.

CHAPTER 25

*L*ater, when she was alone, Evie examined the room she'd
been given.

Another rotunda with marble columns supporting a
domed ceiling, painted with a scene from the mythology books.
Perseus defeating the odious Kraken. In this rendition Perseus, a
golden-haired muscle-bound young man, held the bloody, multi-
vipered Head of Medusa above him. The Kraken was recoiling
but was depicted as already half transformed, with parts of its
octopus-like limbs cracking and falling into a turquoise ocean.
The art was magnificent. Even the vipers looked real enough to
pop their heads out of the ceiling and hiss at her.

The room had no doors or walls. On one side, pure white
curtains hung between each column, billowing in the tender,
fragrant breeze. On the other, beside Evie's decadently comfortable bed, they were held open by gold and ivory hooks carved
into cupped hands. Beyond ancient willows and fields of
Asphodel and daffodils, the sunset was a breathtaking, soul-
calming sight.

Evie lay on the bed, bathed in the brilliant burnt-orange rays
of an Elysian sunset. She basked in its golden warmth while

threading Kampe's stinger between her fingers, threading it through and around each digit, lost in thought. She shook her head at the stray thought which popped in to remind her of that almost deadly miscalculation. The infant had been the Pearl. Evie could always trust her judgment, her instinct was always right. But where had that instinct gone when Evie had battled Kampe and retrieved the baby?

Evie shook her head again. Her judgment was so totally off, she was beginning to wonder if she was Warrior material any longer. She had been so sure the child was innocent. So sure she had almost risked Gavriel's life to save the creature. Almost. Berating herself now was pointless and usually Evie didn't resort to dwelling on the past, but the stinger was a physical reminder of her failure.

She deliberately kept her eyes off her now bare forearms. Clothed in some toga-like garment, Evie felt very naked. Especially with the Mark so revealed to any passing eye. The Mark had not faded. Still black as night and almost alive, the swirling whorls of script and markings were a brutal reminder that even though she was the rightful Ruler of the Underworld, she had been powerless and ignorant when it came to Kampe's deadly child. Ignorant and so naive.

Evie lay back, head sinking into the soft down of the pillow. She was so very tired. She and Gavriel had traveled such a long way to get to the Judgment Hall. She'd faced her mortality in the lava river making her way across the stone steps. She had barely survived the battle with Kampe and who knew where she would be now had Hecate not aided her.

She hadn't had the chance to explain to Gavriel about Hecate revealing her true self. How had he known that the bird would help her? And did he know the bird was Hecate in disguise? And why would Hecate want to help Evie in the first place? What could she possibly gain? So many pieces to this puzzle, none of which seemed to fit together. The Marks moved at the edge of her vision and Evie was reminded that their time in Elysium, and in Tartarus itself, was limited. She had to return to perform the reversal, forsaking her right to the throne. The only thing to be done was to get stronger so she could get out of there, see Daniel and get back to Julian to put things back in order.

Julian who would wait in vain if she lost herself to the beauty of this place. Evie rose from the pillow, slow and steady. She swung her feet to the floor, this time taking it really slow. Now seated, her head spun and the world tilted precariously. Dania had left her a lunch of roast pork and vegetables which now threatened to rise from her belly. Evie gripped the edge of the bed, holding onto her position and her lunch. It would be a shame to lose such a delicious meal. She recalled her amazement that such delicacies were to be found this deep in the Underworld.

At last, when her head stopped spinning and her meal settled back where it belonged, she edged forward and slowly rose to her feet, a tiny inch at a time. Aeon's went by, stars died and whole species became extinct, but at last she was standing upright, on trembling limbs whose muscles quivered in rebellion against her weight. Her head still swam but at least she was conscious.

She breathed slowly, forcing herself to relax. She remained standing, avoiding any pressure on her injured thigh, until she could bear it no longer. With a sigh she collapsed back onto the mattress. Exhausted. Pathetic. Even her leg throbbed despite her care not to stand on it. How was she supposed to confront an Archangel when she could barely stand on her own two feet. There was only one thing to do then - get strong, get past this inability to move around. She hated being stuck in bed, hated being coddled.

Evie lay back and rested for a few minutes then sat up again, rising to her feet. No faster than before, but more sure that she was going to stand up and not keel over into unconsciousness. This time her lunch stayed put. Within half an hour she was strong enough to stand up almost immediately, and had to remind herself to pace herself. As much as her desire to get out of Elysium was strong, her need to get well was stronger. She could not afford a set-back.

Not now. So, easy does it.

During her exercise routine darkness had fallen. Torchlight flickered outside the room. Evie rose to close the curtains at the foot of her bed, then thought better of it and lay back. She was supposed to be recovering, not pushing herself to heal too fast. She planned to regain her strength and leave before Gavriel insisted he had to come with her.

Watching him and his wife together had made her realize how special every moment was that he was able to spend in her company. Evie was certain that once he left Elysium, he wouldn't be able to return. And with the crimes he'd committed in his angelic lifetime he would never gain access to Elysium.

So for now she would play the patient. Then she would be able to leave and be back without disturbing Gavriel's time with Dania.

Two days later Evie was exercising again. Once seated she flexed and relaxed her injured foot, almost passing out on the first go. Her muscles were cramped, tight. Felt almost twisted like someone had gone in and tied fisherman's knots with her muscles. She was sorely tempted to remove the white bandage but the last thing she wanted was to alert anyone.

Besides, Gavriel hadn't come by to see her for two days; no doubt enjoying his sojourn with his wife. Was he reluctant to be reminded that the time he spent here was only temporary? Dania brought her meals, and tended to her wound. Despite her gentleness Dania had a stubborn streak a mile wide. Every time she visited she tried to pull Evie into the conversation. Mundane things like the weather here in Elysian compared to the Upper World, and the architecture and even the painting on the ceiling of her room. She learned a lot about this beautiful place, not that she wanted to. But although Evie smiled and was polite, she wasn't ready to talk. But it seemed Gavriel had spoken to his wife about Evie.

Dania glided through the billowing curtains, the sun casting a halo around her head. She bore a smile and a tray of sticky sweet pastries. She set the tray on Evie's lap and sat beside her legs, giving her knee a small pat. "Gavriel told me you knew Patrick?" She leaned forward eager for Evie's answer.

Evie stiffened. The mere thought of her mentor disturbed the bed of emotions she'd buried deep inside of her heart. It hurt to talk about him but Dania's innocent eagerness put Evie in a difficult position. She could avoid the topic and insult Dania or she could talk and dredge up memories better left alone.

When Evie opened her mouth, having decided to choose avoidance, she immediately shut it. It must have been the serenity of Dania's smile. In it she saw no subterfuge, no hidden agenda. Just a pure need to talk about a mutual friend. And Evie found herself unable to deny her.

"Yes. Patrick was my mentor. He was my guardian and the best father a girl could ever have," Evie said.

Dania nodded, her curls bouncing around her face. "Yes, Patrick had that aura around him. Of one with much love to give."

Dania's words reminded Evie of the first time she'd flown and Patrick's reaction. "You know, when Gavriel left me with him he forgot to mention to Patrick that I was of the angelic persuasion."

Dania nodded. "That sounds like Gavriel." She shared a secretive smile with Evie.

"So the day I first flew must have come as a huge shock to Patrick but he took it in his stride." Evie laughed. "I'd sprouted wings from nowhere and just began to fly off into the sky. Poor

Patrick. He held on for dear life and managed to bring me back down to the ground."

"I bet he was more concerned about your shock than his own," she said.

Evie nodded. "Exactly. He soothed my terror and never once made me afraid or ashamed of my wings. We learned about my angelic side together and he never judged me."

"That was Patrick." Dania sighed. "I knew him through Gavriel but he never judged me either. I was always afraid of what people were saying - those that knew of Gavriel's true nature and of the sin we committed. But Patrick loved that we loved each other. He was all love and no judgment."

"And that was his downfall." Evie's voice was hard as she spoke the words, revealing an anger she'd held for a long time.

Dania's smiled disappeared. "Why do you say that, Evangeline?"

"Because if he'd had the sense to judge Marcellus and Daniel the way they deserved to be judged then he might still be alive today. I went to him repeatedly, warning him of things I'd seen, of my gut instinct, but he chose to believe the monsters were angels."

Dania snorted. "That would surely be difficult when the angels turn out to be monsters."

Evie laughed softly. "That is so true." She sighed. "You're right. I shouldn't be angry with him for his nature. But ..."

"I understand, Evie. You need him now more than ever and he isn't there. Grief is not an easy burden to bear. But you must find a way to forgive him. You must allow him to rest in peace."

Evie frowned. "You think he knows I am troubled?"

Dania nodded. "I believe so. Souls who have passed on retain a connection to their loved ones. They will sense anger and grief in those they left behind. And that will not allow them to rest. You must forgive him to allow him to be at peace."

Evie knew Dania spoke the truth. She nodded. "I will try although it won't be easy. I miss him terribly."

"It takes time but eventually it does get better."

Evie smiled.

The woman had found her weak spot. So they began to talk. First about Patrick and her days growing up with him. Then about her quest to find her father and her double disappointment. About the traitorous Marcellus and the Warriors who were her friends. Before long Evie realized she'd given in to Dania. Perhaps this was why she had remained wife to an Archangel? Only a strong woman could live with Gavriel. And beneath that sublime exterior lay a woman of steel.

So this was what having a mother would have been like. Evie enjoyed it, though she reminded herself this was temporary. She refused to care about another person that she simply had to leave behind.

Then Dania shifted in her seat and patted Evie's knee. "You should get some rest."

"Before you go, can you tell me something?" When Dania nodded, Evie asked, "How do you get to Tartarus from this part of the Underworld? I know I will go with Gavriel once I am ready but I was curious."

After a moment's hesitation, Dania leaned toward the window and pulled the curtain apart. Then she pointed at a rotunda that sat high up on a distant hilltop, surrounded by rose bushes filled with riotous color. "That rotunda is a portal to the Pits. Gavriel will take you when you are stronger. Now you must rest."

Long after Dania left, Evie continued to stare at the rotunda on the hill. Her doorway to the Pits.

The Pits, where Daniel was being held.

CHAPTER 26

*E*vie arrived at the entrance to the Pits, sword at her side, dagger in her boot, expecting a fight. A bit deflated, she was met by a fairly disagreeable creature, almost a minotaur, but not as large or as hungry as she'd expected. He watched her with glossy black eyes as she made her way up the stone pathway and closer to him. His horns gleamed in the light of the flickering torchlight that stood on either side of an entrance guarded by two sullen sentries, who held their spears close.

"How may I help you?" the minotaur asked in a sultry voice that was exceedingly odd and didn't mesh with his furred features at all. He glared at her coldly, as he waited for her response. He wore a black shirt open to the waist, a pair of tan leather pants and sturdy leather boots. In his hand he held a whip which he kept curled around his fingers, as if he was likely to shuck it out and use it in the next second.

He looked at Evie long and hard and just when she was about to squirm he spun on his heel and went to the entrance. He sent word with the sullen sentry for a guard to escort her to see Daniel. The minotaur returned to his post, and stood arms akimbo, as if waiting and ready for the next trespasser.

The guard arrived before Evie could become impatient. He was equally helpful and bustled her along, respectfully bowing his head at all times. He wore a white knee-length chitin that bared one muscle-bound shoulder. His deep blue eyes were watchful and held an expression of concern that Evie would not expect from a mere guard.

She kept her gaze averted and followed at the guard's heels. Evie swallowed nervously. She had not been expecting to be nervous. Soon, they were descending into a deep chasm. Tiny craters dotted the floor of the chasm where figures moved within each pit, wrenching at the chains which bound them, yelling obscenities or just screaming the blood-curdling scream of the demented. It didn't help that the air was choked with the odor of unwashed bodies, and bodily wastes. And something else that Evie wasn't sure she wanted to know.

Black stone walls and pervading darkness made the pits far too eerie to allow Evie to relax. The path they took curved down, hugging the wall until they reached the bottom. From here the pits were much larger in size, with the walls of the little craters at least four times taller than Evie's height including wings. Somewhere in this warren of craters they had stashed the Archangel.

Almost there. It was almost over.

Coming to see Daniel was akin to the purging of her sins. Gavriel had demanded a reason for her fool-hardly intention. Why did she want to do this? At the time she'd had no answer, had been following her instinct. Even now she wasn't so sure. It was more an instinctive need, than a conscious desire. The fact was that Archangel Daniel was her legitimate progenitor. *Father* was not a word she would want to utter in reference to the dark angel she had battled.

The angel who had been so keen on killing her.

Her feet slowed of their own accord. Would have come to a total stop except Evie and her escort had to slip aside in the narrow passage, allowing a cloaked figure to pass by. Cloaked figures were not unusual here in the depths of the underworld. Evie could see a few more walking up ahead, retaining their anonymity within the folds of shadowed hoods. But there was something familiar about the figure that had passed Evie. Perhaps it was the sense that it was a woman hidden beneath the folds of the drab linen.

At the very least it distracted Evie, until she was suddenly at the entrance of the pit serving as a prison for Daniel. She stood in the middle of hundreds of other pits, conveniently roofless so the prisoners could be policed at all times. A black wrought iron gate sealed the entrance of Daniel's prison. Another minotaur was on guard. He stared at Evie and her escort as if contemplating whether to allow Evie through. Then, rattling his keys, he clanked the gate open. He turned his eyes to the floor, but his curiosity was obvious as Evie could feel his eyes follow her into the pit.

The scenery here would never change. Black rock, oil torches, the cloying odor of death and something stale. Her escort said nothing, just indicated for Evie to enter and positioned himself inside the gate. Safety first. Or Julian would have something to say. Inside the cell, darkness warred with the four torches flickering around the prisoner, despite the lack of a roof to the cell. Gavriel had certainly received the better bargain in the scheme of things. When Evie had first seen Gavriel he had been fairly clean, despite the bloody nature of his injuries.

Daniel on the other hand was as soiled on the outside as his black heart surely was on the inside.

His hair was matted and hung unkempt around his face. Evie knew for certain she would not get too close, just to avoid anything that may currently reside within those filthy strands. Her heart gave a plaintive wail - why could her father not have been Gavriel. Good, kind Gavriel who would never have wanted to hurt her the way Daniel had. In this moment before she met his eyes she recalled so vividly the battle in which he'd intended to take her life. And then the moment when she had realized that she had lived on the same estate for an entire decade with Daniel without ever knowing who he was. That he was actually the father she'd been searching for all her life.

Daniel moved his head. He knew someone was here to see him but refused to allow that visitor the satisfaction of his immediate attention. Arrogant. The squalor of his pit teased the bile within her gut. For the briefest second Evie wanted to run. To take flight, admit it was a mistake to want to confront Daniel. Leave it all as it was before. Try and forget it.

But it would never work.

Evie had known it all along. And despite their adamant demands to the contrary both Gavriel and Julian had known she was right. Or that there was at least something justified in her desire to meet the Archangel face to face.

He lifted his head and smiled. A cold, calculating smile so out of place in his filth-ridden face. He hung in the middle of the room from arms raised heavenward and bound by heavy chains. The kind which held Cerberus. The chains were wrapped around his arms, lifting them upward, holding them in permanent supplication to his God. In constant begging for His forgiveness. The muscles in his arms were taut with the strain. But where was the remorse for his actions? And Evie could not find a single iota of pity for his situation. She felt no sadness at his discomfort, no pain at his agony. What should a daughter feel for a father who would let her be killed in cold-blood?

"So, Nephilim. To what do I owe the pleasure of this visit?" His words dripped coldly from his lips, the arrogant curve of a filthy eyebrow a sad shadow of his previous glory.

"My mother. Who was she?" Evie spat the question at him.

Daniel did a double-take, startled at both her directness and at the question.

"How would I know who your mother was, Nephilim? I do not consort with your kind." He smiled, then nodded. "Except of course for all your Warriors of Irin. That was a job, really. Not a choice."

Evie stayed silent, waiting for an answer. She was not about to give up her advantage.

"Now what was this about your mother, Nephilim?" He seemed curious now.

"Who was she? I want her name, her family details. Tell me everything." Evie circled Daniel as he swayed on his chains, especially slowly when she got behind him. The coiling of the muscles in his back confirmed he disliked having her out of his view.

"How would I possibly know who the harlot was that bore you, Nephilim?" When she rounded on him she saw he was smirking again. Someone ought to tell him it's not exactly an expression you can pull off when you look like you've just been dragged through a pile of shit.

Fury surged through Evie's veins. "Because she was your wife, Archangel," she spat, reveling in the darkening of his face. His eyes themselves shifted to a demonic oiliness at her words. But he was good. He recovered well.

"I have had many females in my time, half-breed. How do you expect me to remember the names of every one of them?"

"How many of them did you pledge your vows to?" This time the skin beneath the grime blanched.

"Nephilim," Daniel roared, spittle flying. "How dare you soil the memory of my wife with these questions? My wife was pure when we married. And Sorcha had only one child. That child is dead." He stared at her, almost daring her to deny his words.

"I'm afraid that child is very much alive." Evie took a step toward him. "I know because I am that child."

Evie watched his face. She was sure that he would explode at the news, try and wrench himself from his iron fetters to get at her. But he did nothing. Just hung there, watching Evie, a look of strained grief on his face. Soon enough the expression vanished beneath his usual cool armor. And the tiny pull of empathy she'd felt for his grief disappeared like smoke on the wind.

"So who has spun this story for your benefit, Nephilim?" he asked softly. "Who has whispered little lies in your ears? You want a powerful Archangel as a father, do you?"

"I don't think anyone would manufacture such a tale because they want to be *your* child. Nor would anyone lie about such a thing to me. The thought that you could be my father is as abhorrent to me as the knowledge that you did nothing when the Control came for my mother," she spat, her lip curling in disdain.

"It was inevitable, you know. She knew it. I knew it. So we enjoyed what time we had together." He almost sounded wistful. Until she looked at his black eyes.

"So she survived birthing your child only for you to throw her to the wolves as soon as they came baying at the door? You have no feelings, no heart," Evie said coldly, shaking her head, unable to stomach the thought that anyone could be so callous, so unfeeling.

"Ah, but you forget, Nephilim. Angels are not meant to be emotional creatures. I took a wife, yes. That means nothing, really." If his hands were free Evie was certain he would be doing something arrogantly mundane like inspecting his fingernails or brushing non-existent lint off his shoulders. But he hung from the chains, swathed in excrement, still swaying slightly as he waited for her to respond. And he was waiting, his entire body strained and alert.

Interesting. Maybe the truth did hurt him, maybe the past still had power over him.

But she refused to allow her guard to drop just because he'd revealed a flicker of emotion. It's not as if she'd come to see him to obtain a pledge of undying love.

"I didn't expect anything less from you." She spoke the words with a little lift of her chin.

"Really? Then why did you come here then? What was it you

expected me to say? Hello, my darling child, so glad you dropped by?" His eyes narrowed, growing colder and darker. The pit seemed to close in on Evie, threatening to swallow her whole. Perhaps there was a tiny bit of truth to his taunts. Perhaps a tiny splinter of her heart wanted him to accept who she was. To say she looked like her mother. To say he was sorry he didn't save her. To say he had cared. "You wasted your time, little Nephilim. To me you are nothing. You mean nothing, Half-Breed. I am an Archangel. We do not have weaknesses."

Then he began to shine.

Like a white flame flickering within his body, his skin glowed, even the dirt and grime was unable to hide the power of the light. Incongruously bright for such a black soul. Evie blinked, sure this was not supposed to happen down here. Sure his powers would have been bound before he was brought to the pit.

Something was terribly wrong.

Behind her, Evie heard the guard gasp, then whimper in the glare of the light. Something sizzled, like meat on a hot pan. The stench of cooked flesh burned Evie's nostrils. She heard shuffling, then the gate clanged opened and her guard fled, leaving her alone with the Archangel and his deadly light. A light which clearly had a terrible effect on the inhabitants of the pits. From somewhere above Evie could hear shouts ring out. The guards, seeing the light, were now fleeing.

Let's hope they are scrambling to come and help me, Evie thought wryly. It is possible they just wanted to escape being burnt?

Behind Daniel, his wings crackled, then rose high above him. Pure white and glowing with the same light that shone like a beacon. How unfair it was that this creature, with his incredibly stunning beauty, was evil personified. It didn't seem right. Chains rattled and then there were no chains at all. They lay in crumpled heaps at his sides, reminiscent of a pile of dead vipers, melting in heaps of orange-flecked iron.

Daniel was supposed to be bound by warded chains, chains that prevented his escape, chains that bound his wings.

No, somehow, he was free.

Evie forgot to breathe.

Trapped.

She was trapped.

CHAPTER 27

*A*ny move toward the door would be a waste of time.

She stood in the white shadow of an Archangel who cared nothing that she was his child. A vicious iciness shone from his eyes, the only places still as black as his evil heart. They circled each other, mimicking their actions of their last meeting. This time there was no Gavriel to save her sorry hide. Back in Elysium, Gavriel would be happy with Dania while she met an insignificant death at her father's hand. It seemed macabre but she knew some animals would commit infanticide if they sensed there was something wrong with their offspring. And Daniel certainly looked upon Evie as an abomination. She didn't need reminding of it.

So she played the game, performed the steps to this pitiful death dance, keeping her distance and postponing her end mere seconds. He could have killed her by now. She was no match for him, so she hadn't bothered to shuck her wings. But now, as she moved, a foot to the left, a foot more to the left, she needed some kind of security. Just something to make her feel that much stronger. That much more in control. Besides, she would prefer to welcome her death while her wings were revealed, in all its own silver white glory.

THEY RUSTLED at her back and thrust out behind her in a sudden shower of white glitter. Evie breathed again, releasing the tightness at her chest. Daniel watched a moment, then opened his hand and a silver sword appeared, hilt fitting into his palm like a glove. Evie tasted the malignant poison of death. Her dagger and her sword were no match for this powerful creature. But they were the only weapons she had so grabbed for them and them ready, forcing herself to become part of them, calming her racing heartbeat.

Then, as if bored with the dance, as if impatient for the next move, Daniel raced at her. His speed was phenomenal, but so was her own. As he advanced she ran to the right, using the carved out stone walls for leverage. She ran up the wall, somersaulted over his head and landed behind him. It was showmanship that she could only hope would unsettle him. It was a waste of time. Daniel smiled, then slowly began to rise off the ground.

He seemed to have a thing for fighting in the air.

Evie was tempted to keep the fight on the ground, maybe regain some advantage since he seemed to much at home fighting in the air. But the thought that he may change his mind and try to escape Tartarus made her stomach twist.

She could not let him escape his prison.

So, Evie rose too, and met him face to face, still keeping a safe distance from the glowing sword. His laughter rang out as he thrust his sword toward Evie's chest with lightning speed. It sliced through the air, and though Evie tried to parry the blow, Daniel's sword went through her arm like butter. The power behind the sword was so powerful that it sang a song that resonated in Evie's mind. He pulled his blade free and her blood spilled from the slashed skin, dripping onto her boots and onto the ground now several feet below them. She could not risk holding her arm even if it meant she could stop the flow of the blood from the wound. So she put the icy pain and the threatening dizziness out of her mind and gripped her weapons, concentrating on battling this demon in Heaven's garb.

They fought, thrusting, parrying. A visceral battle which sent them spinning in a vortex of hate and disappointment, anger and pain. Weaker now, she had to concentrate harder as a swipe of the sword took off a chunk of her hair and almost sliced her scalp open. Somewhere in her mind Evie laughed at the picture of Ash scolding her for being so careless that she would endanger her beautiful tresses.

Another somersault over the angel landed her behind Daniel lightning fast. Quick enough to thrust her silver dagger deep between his ribs. Deep red, almost black blood spilled from the wound when she tugged her dagger from his flesh. Evie wasted no time, not trusting that the injury she caused would slow the Angel down. She swooped below him, narrowly missing the stream of still-steaming blood as it trickled to the stone floor. She was vaguely conscious of the increase in the volume of the noise around her. Vaguely aware that the fresh hot blood of her father now mingled with her own cooling droplets on the floor of the pit.

Daniel swooped down on her again. And this time she didn't have the strength to escape. She was too slow. Loosing blood had slowed her reflexes. The edge of Daniel's blade was so fine that Evie didn't feel the skin on her thigh split open. Not until her leg warmed with blood that dripped from her flesh did she register the newest injury.

Daniel smiled.

Nothing fatherly at all about his grin. Throughout the battle he'd been so silent. And Evie had played his game. Not wanting to be seen as weak, not wanting him to win the power play.

"Are you ready to give up, *Daughter*?" He spoke the word as if he said Demon. Perhaps to him they were not very different. Angels considered Nephilim to be the preferred species of their offspring with humans, but only a few genes away from their demon cousins.

"Not yet, *Father*." Evie injected as much, if not more, disdain and disgust into the word. This time taking pleasure from the scowl that darkened his face.

"Do not call me that, Half-Breed," he bellowed. It was the feather that tipped his scales.

He flew at her, in a fury that compared little to Kampe's vicious anger when Evie had stolen her little scorpion baby. Evie had no defenses now, no strength left to defend herself. She just waited for death to come.

But something large and dark swooped down on them. Evie blinked and looked up, gazing at the movement. It felt like time had slowed as she watched the progress of the dark form above. From the corner of her eye she saw Daniel was getting closer and closer, the sword shimmering in the angel light, the sharp edge drenched with her blood. Daniel's eyes swirled with black anger, so much that even the whites of them were tainted with smoky darkness. His lips curved in a vicious smile as his teeth were revealed at the corners of his mouth.

Then Gavriel swooped down at Daniel, hitting him broadside, the glowing sword glowing no longer as it left Daniel's palm, spun across the pit and clattered to the ground. Daniel was tossed against the far wall, his head bouncing off the jagged rock as he bumped to the dirt floor. Gavriel hovered between Evie and the Dark Angel, protecting her from any reprisal. Evie's head spun, but within the haze of it she recognized the sword lay unguarded on the stone below. The two angels stared at each other, neither paying attention to Evie.

Good.

She could use that to her advantage. She lowered herself to the ground, her knees crumbling beneath her, unable to hold her body weight not to mention the added weight of her wings. She let go of her own weapons and reached out her hand, curling a finger around the hilt of Daniel's sword and tugged. All the while she kept her eye on the two angels who stared each other down, both furious but for very different reasons.

Evie flinched as the sword spun on the hilt instead of sliding toward her. This weapon was gleaming silver, thin and not very long. Very different to Daniel's angelic obsidian sword. She glanced quickly at the pair. Still safe. She lunged forward and gripped the sword, curling her fingers around the hilt. She held on tightly and rose to her feet. The sword of the archangel hung heavy at her left hip, so heavy that lifting it to point upward at her side was so strenuous she saw stars at the edges of her vision and almost passed out. She'd seen Ling do that with her thin serrated blade, keep it flush against her body, to use it in a surprise attack because her opponent could not see it hidden at her side.

She had meant to fly back upward and join the fight, although she had no idea how she intended to surprise Daniel with a new opening in his flesh.

But it never happened.

He was at her right side before she blinked. Even blinking seemed to take twice the amount of time in her blood-drained state, but she tried to stay as aware as she could. Didn't want to miss the moment of her demise. She would have laughed if she'd had the strength. Daniel reached out and gripped her head in his hands, her chin lay in the palm of one hand, and she felt the strength of the other hand at the back of her head.

Lovely, how nice to die with a quick twist of the neck. Not a glamorous ripping open by a sharp blade. A twist of the neck.

He remained at her right side, unaware of the sword she held at her left shoulder. Gavriel swooped down from above but slowed in his approach when he registered the danger she was in.

"Leave her, you bastard," he shouted.

"I gave her life, and I can take it away," the dark angel yelled back, bristling with energy and anger. Daniel's fingers dug into the skin of her chin, reminding her of his deathly grip. Then he squeezed tighter and turned her face away from him, so she faced his nemesis.

Evie blinked, and even her eyelids felt too heavy for the action. She tipped her head slightly to watch them and realized too that this was the moment she'd been waiting for. With the two angels locked in a battle of anger and stares, with her life hanging in the balance, what time was better to make her move.

At her side, out of sight of Daniel, she tilted the sword backward until its tip almost touched the flesh beneath his ribs. Her arm was angled at Daniels torso behind, ready to strike. His grip tightened on her head and she knew beyond a shadow of doubt that he meant to end her life in that moment. Not to punish Gavriel for his love of her, but just for the pure satisfaction of it. She took her chance and shoved upward as hard as she could, using all the energy left within her body, her mind and her soul.

She felt the blade sever organs as it ripped through his body, felt the slight resistance when the point reached the thicker flesh of his heart, felt the hard outside wall break in a rush of blood.

When his grip loosened on her head Evie was unaware she had succeeded. Stunned and in shock from blood-loss, she was slightly dizzy. Only when Gavriel came and grabbed her hand within his warm fingers did she blink some awareness into her mind. He gripped her hand that still held the hilt of the sword. Behind her, Daniel had fallen, his momentum freeing him from the sword, but the damage had been done. The blade had pierced his heart of hearts.

The final death blow.

Patricide.

The highest of sins. The word hit Evie like a blow to her own heart. She must have breathed the word out loud as Gavriel's face darkened. His feathers answered and darkened to almost black. "Don't you ever think that. He may have sown the seed that became you but he was no father to you."

Evie stared at Gavriel's face. The passion in his eyes glowed. He really believed those words. Words that made her feel better, that made her want to believe him. She could not agree with him yet. So she just nodded, not trusting herself to speak. She needed to work out what she felt about killing her Father, her own flesh and blood. Evie turned to stare at the shell of the Archangel.

He no longer glowed with the bright, blinding, heavenly light. The body shimmered and a shadow rose.

So Angels did have souls.

Daniels spirit rose and hovered over his body. His smile, even his demeanor was as arrogant in death as he had been in life. But his smile faltered then died when a woman appeared in the pit. She was more shadow than corporeal. White hair flowed over her shoulders, and her eyes were all white, no pupil, just pearly white. And *she* did not smile. She inclined her head in greeting to both Evie and Gavriel, then stood waiting. Daniel's face paled in utter horror.

Evie glanced at Gavriel. Even in her weakened state, curiosity still overcame her. He mouthed 'Fury', then turned his attention back to Daniel's spirit. The dark angel may have intended to put up a fight. Perhaps he'd intended to escape from the Fury, but he should have known it was inevitable.

She held out a pale hand, creased palm up. And though Daniel screamed and shook his head, the expression on his face turning a once handsome angel into something ugly, something horrible. He screamed again but nobody heard him. His spirit was like smoke, and it swirled in an eddy as the Fury coaxed him into her palm. Like a tornado, the shade of the Archangel Daniel spun on the palm of the Fury's hand, and then disappeared into nothing in the blink of an eye.

Evie sighed in relief. Then sighed again when the Fury nodded in greeting and disappeared in a puff of spirit smoke.

She would have sighed again, but instead, she fainted.

CHAPTER 28

*E*vie opened her eyes to find herself back in Elysium. Her heart fell, disappointed she wasn't back with Julian in Hades. But Elysium was surely a better option than the Pits of Tartarus. Her arm and thigh were numb but her thigh stung as if a thousand bees had decided to simultaneously dive-bomb the injured limb. She twisted her foot hoping the movement would stop the stinging, but all it did was send agony shooting up her thigh.

"Do not wriggle. You will open the wounds again," Gavriel's nagging was soft and soothing. She huffed and turned her head to look at the welcome sight of his face. She threw him a sheepish smile. "You are not the easiest patient to tend."

"Sorry. I'll try to be good," Evie said, swallowing against the lump in her throat. "How long have I been out?"

"Two days." Gavriel leaned forward, the frown on his face saying what his mouth wouldn't. "What you need to do is get better. If you want to hand the mantle back to Julian you had better get well. Fast. We only have a few more days and a long way to go."

There was an urgency in his voice that brought reality slamming back down on Evie. "How long have I been out?"

"Only a few hours," he said reassuringly.

"Feels like days." Evie lay back on the soft pillow and exhaled. She shifted, enjoying the warmth of the sun on her cheeks.

"You lost a lot of blood. Drained, you were." He was trying to make light of the whole incident. Trying not to make her think about killing Daniel. But he hadn't had a hope to begin with. She swallowed. The world was likely better off with him gone, but Evie wasn't thrilled to be the one who dispatched him.

"So how is our patient?" Dania's voice filtered past Gavriel's body and she poked her hand through the crook of his elbow to smile at Evie.

"She needs to get better, that is how she is," he said, gruffly, scowling.

Dania punched him lightly on the shoulder and mimicked his scowl. "Well she will not get better with you around mister thunder cloud. Take that scowl and go away." She spoke sweetly. Still, the iron was there. He rose and gave her a tender glance before leaving without a fuss. "That man has not changed at all."

She shook her head and sat down beside Evie. "Are you well my dear?" Evie met her eyes, saw that she was not asking about her health. The state of her heart and her conscience did not seem likely to change very soon. "What you did today ... killing Daniel ... that took courage."

Evie nodded, trying to look at it from Dania's perspective. "I was just defending myself ... And Gavriel. I didn't go in there intending to kill him."

Dania patted Evie's arm. "You do not have to justify what you did. Not to me, not to anyone. He threatened your life and you defended it. Your life or his - simple as that."

"Still patricide as far as I can see." Evie's eyes filmed with tears and she couldn't look at Dania, couldn't meet her eye, too afraid of seeing the revulsion within them. Instead Dania grabbed her arm and shook her, uncaring that the wound on Evie's hand was just inches from her thumb.

"Never say that. Ever." Anger burned in Dania's eyes. "You did not kill your father. The man you killed was an Archangel with a black heart. One who would have killed you without a speck of conscience. He did not raise you. He did not care for you. He taught you nothing, helped you with nothing. Do not give him in death what you refused him in life. Do not give him power over you. If you do, then he wins. Then ... he wins."

The words, backed with such unadulterated passion, rang in Evie's ears. She just wanted to block it out, roll over and sleep. Try to forget everything that happened.

"Oh no, you do not get to do that. I know that look. You are not allowed to give up." Dania sat before Evie, gripping the Nephilim's chin in her fingers. "Look at me. You are not allowed to give up. There is too much at stake. You need to get back to Hades, and so does Gavriel. Neither of you can stay here for much longer. So cease feeling sorry for yourself."

Dania bent to the floor and lifted a bowl, removing its white linen cover. She swirled the golden liquid inside it, around and around.

Pure gold. Manna.

"Drink this. It will help you heal. Help your wounds and give you strength." Dania didn't wait for Evie to resist. She placed the bowl to Evie's lips and lifted it. A silent threat that Evie submitted to. *Drink, or else.*

So Evie drank deeply, and found herself reveling in the taste of sunshine and happiness and pure unadulterated bliss on her tongue. She lay back, languid and relaxed, wanting to stretch and yawn and curl up to sleep and dream. Of course, she didn't allow the stretching for fear of opening wounds, new and old. But she did yawn and curl up to sleep.

～

A FEW HOURS LATER, Evie awakened, refreshed and with a clear head. Gavriel stood by the window, staring out at something as the breeze played with the silken curtains. She found Dania at her side, stiff and still, as is she'd been waiting a while.

And she certainly didn't waste any time. She rose the moment Evie's eyes opened and said, "Right, you are ready." She patted Evie's satchel, and flipped it open to reveal the bulging contents; food for the trip back up to Hades. Evie swung her legs off the bed and found she had plenty of her old strength back. She sighed, so ready to leave. Dania laughed softly. "I would say come back soon, but..." She gave a mischievous grin and stepped back.

Gavriel opened his arms to his wife and she stepped into them, enfolded and all but disappearing within the bear hug. Evie blinked back tears at the sight, then averted her eyes. She felt like an intruder watching their last embrace.

Finally, Dania sniffed and drew back. Then she unclasped a pendant from around her neck. She walked to Evie and fastened it around her. Both Gavriel's and Dania's eyes glittered with tears. Evie wasn't sure what to say so she kept silent. Words seemed far too trivial for such a gift.

She touched the pendant and leaned forward to place a kiss on Dania's soft cheek. When she and Gavriel stepped through the curtained doorway, neither could bear to look back at Dania, standing alone in the now empty rotunda with sun shining in her hair, and tears gleaming in her eyes.

Goodbye Dania, Evie whispered.

THEY'D BEEN RISING up the black tunnel for almost two hours before Gavriel cleared his throat. "The children were not killed. The Control took them. It was only the mothers who were slaughtered." Evie listened in shocked silence. Her mother too. "They took the bodies of the children away and because everyone knew they burned the bodies of any Nephilim they found, we never looked for them. But she lives. Our child lives." The despair in his voice was an almost tangible thing and brought tears to Evie's eyes.

She swallowed hard. What could she say to this Revelation? It should have made him happy, instead he wept as he spoke. Air rush against their faces as they rose up through the earth, following the meandering tunnel.

"These are for you." He reached into his pocket and opened his palm. She saw two more pendants, so similar to the one Dania had placed around her neck that she didn't need to compare them. She had already traced the pendant so many times she had the pattern imprinted in her memory. They were identical. "These are given to our children. It was a tradition started by a few angels who had forsaken their vow by marrying Human women. Each child was given a pendant. Of course, the Control was not aware of the tradition so they didn't think to take the jewelry."

Evie looked at the two pendants glittering in her palm. Warm air brushed her wet cheeks before she realized she'd shed tears for those lost children. "Two?" she asked, but she already knew the answer.

"You had a sister. At the time I'd thought they killed your mother before the babe was borne. Dania told me what really happened."

"How did she know the truth and you didn't?" His face contorted with grief at my question. "Because she was there when it happened. They arrived just after your sister came into the world. Dania tended your mother, birthed the babe and remained by her side. When the Control came they knew who Dania was. They killed her. Then they killed your mother, taking your infant sister away. They didn't think to look for another child as their intelligence would have indicated only one offspring for Daniel. Angels spent many months, even years away from their human families. When I arrived home I found it empty and assumed Dania had brought Alyssa over to play with you. But all I found was you, half starved and almost out of your mind. I knew you needed special care, more than I was able to give you. Patrick was my only option.."

Evie felt a sob grab hold of her throat. That was why all Patrick had known was Evie's mother had died in childbirth. Because even Gavriel himself had been unaware of the birth of the second child. Evie felt her fingers tighten at the horror of her mother's and Dania's deaths. Then she stiffened. Three pendants-one each for her and her sister. And the third? She cleared her throat. "You said 'the children were not killed'? Did they take your child too?

Gavriel dropped his gaze but Evie could see his throat convulse as he struggled with his own grief. "Dania took our daughter with her. Alyssa and you were of the same age. You grew up together, playmates all those years. When the servants warned her of intruders, Dania told you both to hide. She never saw Alyssa again. And when I arrived I only found you."

He fell silent and I didn't want to press him any further. So. I changed the topic. "So they had a plan? The Control? Is there something else bigger happening?" Evie tried not to think about her mother's death. She had not been fortunate enough to see her mother in Elysium. Unlike Gavriel. "Why is my mother not with Dania? In Elysium, I mean?"

He shook his head, grief still darkening his brow. "Sorcha killed one of the angels of the Control. You cannot enter Elysium if you have taken the life of another, regardless of the reasons."

"Sounds unfair." Evie gritted her teeth at the unfairness of the Underworld as a whole.

"It is unfair, but those are the rules."

"So where is she now?" Evie asked. She didn't expect an answer though. Gavriel's attitude would be so different had he known the whereabouts of the stolen children.

And he was shaking his head. "I don't know. So many places. Heaven? Reincarnation? I can't guess and I don't think anyone will tell us either."

"So my boon? The ones the Judges spoke of? This is my boon then?" Gavriel nodded. "A sister. I have a sister." Evie spoke the words, rolling them off her tongue as if testing the idea. Something she had never thought about.

A sister.

CHAPTER 29

*W*alking back into Julian's living room was surreal.

The fire flickered in the grate, its shadows dancing on the walls and the furnishings. The room was a refreshing change from black stone, lava rivers, and deadly scorpion babies.

But it wasn't the room that held Evie's attention. It was Persephone's hand on Julian's face, her nails caressing his cheek dangerously as if any change in mood would lead her to gouge the sharp red tips into his skin. Julian had his back to Evie, the silk of his white shirt lay against the strong muscles of his back. He remained unaware of her entry and Evie held off from announcing her arrival.

Evie watched the goddess. And though the expression in her eyes was far from seductive, Evie's hackles rose. So did her wings. They flared behind her in tandem with her anger.

Beside Evie, Gavriel stiffened and a quick glance at him showed him gulp down his shocked laughter. So he found this scene amusing. Good for him, though Evie, her blood pressure inching sky high.

Persephone turned to the movement at the door. When her

gaze settled on Evie, her face darkened, shock coloring her skin a dusky rose. Evie frowned at the goddess, but Persephone didn't move. She remained frozen with shock, so surprised that Evie had walked into the room that she was lost for words. But it wasn't just Evie's intrusion on her moment with Julian that had shocked the goddess. Something else was going on in the she-wolf's head.

In the moment of silence that followed, a handful of memories tickled at Evie's mind. A cloaked figure in the pits. A strange sense of familiarity. The certainty that the fold of fabric had hidden the form and shape of a woman.

Persephone's swaying walk.

Persephone's flowery perfume.

Evie stiffened when the pieces fell into place. It had been Persephone who had gone to see Daniel ahead of Evie. Persephone who had freed him and put both Evie's and Gavriel's lives in danger. But the goddess had failed.

Miserably.

In the end her ally had been killed. Evie paused a second to consider her enemy's motive. Then she stiffened. In truth, Persephone was not her enemy. She didn't even know the goddess. Persephone's hatred was due to mere circumstance. It was Julian that Persephone seemed to think she owned. Evie's gut tightened. She didn't much like that thought. Persephone had her own husband, never mind that he was prancing around the world on a personal sabbatical.

"Persephone," Evie said softly her eyes never leaving the goddesses face. "I thought I recognized you." Evie's smile was friendly but contained enough venom to kill Kampe herself.

At the sound of Evie's voice, Julian jerked away from the goddess and spun around. "Evangeline, thank the Gods." Julian took two loping steps to her, and folded her into a hug not unlike the one Gavriel had so recently shared with Dania. A hug meant to convey love and care and it should have brought an explosion of joy to her heart knowing how deeply Julian felt for her. But her eyes and focus remained on Persephone whose serene beauty had crumpled in anger. Evie's rigid spine alerted Julian to her mood. "What is the matter? Recognize whom?"

"Oh, I just realized I recognized Persephone from the Pits."

"The Pits?" Julian let go of Evie and turned to stare at the goddess. "What were you doing in the Pits? You made it a rule never to go there." There was dangerous edge to his voice that made Evie accept she didn't truly know the man. Not yet.

"Yes, Julian," Evie answered, her gaze back on Persephone's white face. "I saw Sef at the Pits. Right before I was led into Daniel's cell. Right before I was almost slaughtered by a prisoner who had been mysteriously freed from his chains." While Evie let that statement sink in she noticed the smug satisfaction that filled Persephone's face. Julian would not have missed her expression either. "Oh, and right before I killed the prisoner."

The silence was a vacuum of nothingness.

Persephone's face was cold. And priceless. Her features were contorted in pure and volatile anger. So pure that the wood in every piece of furniture split and cracked apart, as if unable to hand the sudden temperature drop.

Evie felt goose bumps rise on her skin in protest against the sudden cold but she could not care less about Persephone's mood. Evie had dealt her own powerful blow. One that the goddess had not been expecting.

Evie had killed the Archangel and as a result, bested the goddess of springtime.

"What did you do?" Julian addressed Persephone, his tone even colder that the goddesses fury.

"Nothing I was not entitled to do, your Majesty." Persephone smiled but it was frost and ice, and her tone was every bit as condescending and arrogant as Daniel's. "Pity my plan did not work though."

"Get out." Julian pointed at the door, brooking no excuse from her. "I should have you sent back down to Tartarus for this."

Persephone scoffed. "And leave the earth to wallow in the arms of Winter? Really, Julian? I think not. Have you forgotten who I am? I am Mother Nature. I am Spring and Summer. I am the harvest and the grain and the food for the earth." She lifted her chin, tossed her blond curls over her shoulder and walked out, regal, graceful and terribly angry.

"What am I going to do with her?" Julian sighed as he watched Mother Nature leave the room. Then he turned to Evie. "I am so sorry Evangeline. I thought with Gavriel you would be well protected. I hadn't counted on Persephone to force her way into things.

"How did she even get to the Pits and back before us?" asked Evie, frowning.

"Persephone is a goddess of Hades, and has the same powers that I do. She can transport herself to wherever she wishes, anywhere in the world, above or below ground."

"Oh." Evie's eyes narrowed. "Then why didn't you just take me to Tartarus?"

Julian shook her head. "There are some thing I cannot meddle in. You are angelic, and you were travelling with an angel who is technically a prisoner of Hades. I could not help you beyond the little I was able to do. The gods of Judgment had to rule."

I heard his words and understood what he meant.

Then he said, "Something needs to be done about Sef." He spoke the words with such sadness that Evie's heart throbbed in empathy.

"Nothing needs to be done. Persephone is part of the scheme of things, both here in Hades and up on Earth," Evie said as she pushed back the sleeve to reveal the pulsing Marks. "But now, Julian, we have better things to think about than a jealous wife. It's time to end this."

Julian's gaze swiveled to the Marks and he sighed. Evie wasn't sure what that sigh meant as it sounded too sad for a man about to regain his immortality. "Very well, then." Julian spared Evie only one small frown. He glanced at Gavriel who smiled then tapped him a small salute before heading toward Julian's bar.

Then Julian beckoned Evie and led the way.

WHEN JULIAN and Evie reached the Ascension Hall, Evie's stomach did a somersault. She recalled her reaction the first time she'd seen the thick, solid stone door that guarded the entrance. The lintel rose high above her head. Gigantic black metal hinges pinioned the stone door, as large as the muscles in Evie's arms.

She glanced at the doorknob before Julian grabbed onto it. The knob that sat in the middle of the door was only a tiny bit smaller than Julian's own fist. Evie couldn't stop herself from placing her palm flat against the stone door. She'd been ready to feel the pulsing, throbbing from inside the room. Only this time she felt nothing.

Evie gave a mental shrug. Maybe giving back the seals worked differently.

Julian turned the knob, then gave the door an almighty shove before it opened in strange silence. For a door that size it should have made at least a little bit of noise. Evie's thoughts were distracted by the Ascension table in the middle of the room.

It took pride of place in the stark stone room. And this time Evie could feel the power inside of the stone, reaching for her. She felt the pulsing, throbbing softly in her ears, and as before she seemed to move to the side of the table without realizing it.

Evie stared at the centerpiece of the room. The large stone table. A shudder ran up her back as memories filtered through her mind. She shook them away and studied the octagonal table. A round depression was carved out of each of the eight corners. And inside each one lay a Seal, its sweet notes echoing along the stone walls. Evie found that her blood and even her muscles sang the Seal's song.

"You have the final seal?" Julian glanced at Evie, his brow still furrowed.

She nodded and reached the medallion that she'd returned to its place around her neck.

The second her skin touched the medallion the seals around the table began to glow golden. The angelic script engraved into the metal seemed to take on a life of its own, spinning and dancing across the surface of the seal. Each Seal began to slowly spin anti-clockwise and Evie recalled it had spun in the opposite direction when she'd received the Seals not so long ago.

And as before, one symbol on each of the seals shone brightly, each one a different script than the next seal. The singing and the spinning would have begun to make Evie dizzy but she felt her hand begin to move, pulled toward the table by the combined force of all the power of the Seals of Hades.

The last time she'd been here Evie had been dragged bodily across the surface of the table. This time she was determined to avoid losing control. She hopped onto the table and spun around on her butt until she was in position. Then she opened her palm and let the medallion float above her hand. It hesitated only a second before flying upward.

When it paused at the pinnacle of the arrangement, bright white light shot from each of the seals, all aimed to meet at a point just above Evie's medallion. And Evie was now surrounded by white rays, engaged within the light of the Seals.

Evie stared up at the medallion that hovered above her. She'd had it all her life, carried it around with her for centuries. A gift from her father but he hadn't been her father had he? Gavriel had given her the medallion for safe-keeping. She doubted he would ever have thought it would come to this.

Evie blinked and realized the strength of the Seal's song had subsided to a comfortable hum. Everything seemed calm, as if the Seals were waiting for something.

She glanced over at Julian, at his hand where the Mark had faded to a pale memory on his skin. This had to be done. His mortality would come crashing back down upon him. This was the only way to keep him immortal. At last, the sound of the chimes lulled into soft silence.

Black shadows rose from Evie's arm, twisting and writhing in the air, then disappearing into the air above them. Evie kept her gaze on Julian's arm, her heart thudding as she waited. She only exhaled when she saw the Marks re-appear stronger and darker on his forearm. The ritual was almost at an end and Evie tried to breath, to calm herself.

But something was wrong.

The mark had been transferred so Evie's arm should be bare of any dark writing scripts. But they were still there, still strong and dark and still emblazoned on her arm.

The magic gone. Evie hesitated then pushed herself up onto her elbows. She stared from her arm to Julian's, confusion contorting her brow. Then she sat up and stared at her arm.

What in Hades was going on?

"It has been transferred. It is done." Julian's voice rang around the small room, almost triumphant as he gazed at the marks bight and new on his forearm.

"No it has not," Evie answered softly, raising her arm for him to see the Mark.

Julian gasped then shook his head. He walked forward and took Evie's arm in his hand, comparing it to his own forearm. "That is simply not possible. It should have been a clean transfer." Julian stared for a long time. Until his brow smoothed out and confusion left his darkened eyes. "Perhaps it has something to do with your trip into Tartarus and your battle with Kampe. And maybe the killing of Daniel. I believe you have earned the Mark, not just been given it in a ritual."

Evie shook her head, still confused.

"It means you are still Ruler of Hades. Co-ruler, ruler, just words. What you are is the wielder of dominion over the Under-world. As am I." Julian raised his arm and placed it next to hers. A matched pair. It's supposed to be impossible. But there you have it."

Evie smiled. Better to laugh it off than to cry. "Does this mean I don't get to go home?"

Julian shook his head. "There is no precedent here, Evie. I think you can probably do whatever you want."

Evie scanned his face. She lifted her hand, her fingers reaching out to trace his brow. The signs of age, the paleness to his cheeks, even the slight bow of his shoulders were all gone. "You have your immortality back."

"I believe I do." He smiled.

Evie traced the black whorls on her arm. No longer were they abhorrent. Hating them had only been part of her fear for Julian's life. For his lack of immortality because of her stupidity.

Now she had power.

And strength. The past was over, Marcellus and Daniel were gone from the Irin. And if Evie didn't get back soon, Flash would be running things and that was definitely not a good thing.

Evie stood, taking a deep breath and feeling as if it was her first in a very long time.

If the Mark was there to stay, then so was the power. And with power come influence. Evie smiled.

"Now, I can find my sister."

CHAPTER 30

*E*vie emerged into the sunlight and had to immediately shade her eyes. The brightness dazzled her and pain seared into the back of her head. The joys of not having sunglasses. She stepped away from the cave and scanned the surrounding trees and dense vegetation.

Then she sighed. She was home, free of the bounds that held her to the Kingdom of Hades. Despite the markings which gleamed black and fresh on her forearm, Evie felt that a new day was about to begin. One where the brotherhood would face the future led by someone who did not have their own agenda, by someone who had the needs of humanity at heart.

Evie stared up into the bright blue sky. She felt the bones in her back burgeon as her wings sprang forth in a dusting of silver and a puff of pure white feathers. Then she shoved off the ground and soared high into the air, a feeling of exhilaration pulsing through her veins as she banked right and headed for the estate.

A sister.

She never would have known the truth if she hadn't pursued the Seals, so some good had certainly come out of that disaster. But what did she do about the seals now? The Markings pulsed and throbbed on her arm as if they were living breathing creatures, but for now she pushed all thoughts of them out of her mind and concentrated on the one thing that pulsed through her soul - the need to find her sister.

Evie was certain that the Control would have had a more sinister reason for capturing them than just the desire to rid the world of the abomination called Nephilim. And Evie swore that she would find out what that reason was.

Evie scanned the horizon. Greylock was just up ahead, the faint mirage of the protective dome clear to Evie's angelic sight. She inhaled as she pointed her toes for her landing. She couldn't deny the pulse of excitement she experienced, knowing she was coming home to her friends.

Her feet crunched deep into the black gravel that littered the rooftop of the old castle. Constructed of large grey stones, it was reminiscent of something ancient, with a decidedly English air. Giant floor to ceiling windows, archways, and rich old wood gave the building a mysterious yet livable feel.

The gargoyle guard was absent, sending a wave of concern through Evie's chest. What reason would there be for having no watchman up on the roof? Even in broad daylight the guards never left their posts. Evie tried to shrug off her worry, chalking the guard's absence up to changeover or timing. She hurried to the edge of the roof and floated down to the stone-tiled patio below. This one led to the common room where Evie was hoping to see Ling and Ash. She hadn't kept track of the passage of time too well and she suspected the girls would have returned a few weeks ago.

The common room was silent and empty. Again, an unusual thing considering the height of the sun. Lunchtime. The commons should be throbbing with Nephilim right now, all hungry and sociable. Evie's heels tapped the wood floor as she headed out of the common room and down the passage.

At the next turn she hesitated. Should she go up to Marcellus' study hoping to meet his successor or should she go and find the girls first? Evie made up her mind and headed right, reaching the stairs to the upper floor within seconds. Soon she was knocking on Ling's door and receiving no answer. Along the hall she rapped her knuckles on Ash's door. Again, no response.

Frowning Evie hurried to her own room. It certainly looked like the place was deserted but Evie knew that wasn't possible. The brotherhood wouldn't stop their work just because they didn't have a Master. By now they should have chosen a new Master. And things should be rolling along smoothly. But why the strange silence?

Flinging her door open Evie entered the room and headed to her closet. She grabbed fresh clothes and was about to head into the bathroom when a sound at the door caught her attention. Immediately Evie pulled her glamor over her body, just in case. She faced the door, watching it as she stood very still and waited. But the sound didn't come again. Evie shrugged and dropped her glamor.

She turned to enter the small bathroom attached to her room when something smashed hard into her head. So hard that Evie lost her balance. Her body was still recovering from her various wounds and this blow to her head was enough to knock her senseless.

She crumpled into an untidy heap and gave herself up to darkness.

EVIE CAME TO, but when she opened her eyes she couldn't see a thing.

She was seated on something hard. Wood beneath her, wood at her back. A large chair. A cold breeze scraped her cheek as it went by, whistling as it found nooks and crannies to travel through. The sound was enough to wake all the dead of Tartarus.

Evie blinked few times, wondering if the blow to her skull had rendered her sightless. Her eyeballs hurt inside her head but that was more a sign of an aching head than anything else. After a few seconds of staring around her with intense concentration, she found she could make out faint patches of light at the edges of her vision. No, she wasn't blind. She was just somewhere very, very dark.

She raised her hand to touch the throbbing spot on the back of her head but found her wrist bound. The other arm was afforded the same attention. From the soft leather against her skin she imagined the cuff and the straps, the large notches, the old stone prongs. Cuffs used for special prisoners. Prisoners kept in the dungeons deep below the castle.

Evie's heart thudded so loudly that she almost didn't hear the voice.

Her eyes darted blindly around her. "Who's there?" she asked the darkness. The darkness didn't answer.

Then Evie heard it again. But it wasn't the sound of a voice. Someone was at the door. A key scratched in a lock somewhere in front of her. A strip of light appeared, then widened as a huge stone door was pushed open. A hooded figure glided into the room and came to stand two feet before Evie. The figure was back lit, the light at the edge of her captor's head stabbed into Evie's eyes causing them to water. The stark outline of the cowl sent shivers of worry up Evie's spine.

The light fell on Evie's bound wrists but what she saw made her want to pass out again. Angelic script, burnt into every inch of the leather that held her so tightly. Angelic words to bind an angelic being.

Evie tamped down her rising panic. She needed a clear head, she needed calm to deal with this ridiculous situation. "What's going on? Where am I?" Evie asked, injecting her usual cool, unaffected tone into her voice. She would not let them see her afraid, no matter what they did to her.

"You are here the Greylock estate," the voice was soft, elegant and unfamiliar. Evie tilted her head, still having not seen what her visitor looked like, she was now more curious than ever. A hand, disembodied in the dark shadows, emerged from the cloak and pushed the hood back to reveal a mane of tightly curled coal-black hair. Her heart-shaped face was serene and controlled as she met Evie's gaze. Deep brown eyes, caramel skin and a sweet smiling mouth completed the picture of Evie's captor. "My name is Mykia Goodwin. I am the new Master of the Brotherhood of the Irin."

A female Master. Well, well, well. Good for the Brotherhood. About time they ceased their sexist ways. But a thought niggled Evie's mind. What if this woman was just a figurehead just the hand to do the bidding of another? Or what if she was the type to disregard the right and wrong just to prove she deserved her position?

But Evie couldn't waste time thinking about the progression of the rights of women, or the ability of the woman before her to carry out her sworn duty. Right now her own rights were being disregarded. "Why are you holding me?"

"You are awaiting your trial." Mykia's voice remained soft, but it held a note of authority to it. Her brown eyes flashed but her expression was far from judgmental. That didn't mean Evie could trust her.

"What trial? What the hell is going on here?" Frustration brought an edge to Evie's voice. One that came with a low rumble of angelic fury. Immediately she tamped it down but it was probably too late. And it didn't matter. Another rule broken would not be of much concern considering Evie's current position as captive and defendant. "What am I accused of?"

Evie wanted to sob. She'd saved them all from Daniel and Marcellus when they'd been using the brotherhood for his own end. They should be grateful but now *she* was on trial?

Mykia's next words chilled her to her soul.

"You, Evangeline, Nephilim of the Irin, are accused of the highest of treasons."

"And what exactly is this treason?"

"Murder."

— TO BE CONTINUED —

Read the next book in the Irin Series:
Resonance

To Leigh K. Hunt
To a most amazing friend. I'm so grateful for everything you have done
for me. You are simply the best.

ACKNOWLEDGMENTS

To my Inklings girls – thank you for your support, encouragement and love.

To my proofreader Karen Mead, you always work like a demon to help me meet my deadlines- you are amazing.

To my family – For your unfailing support in my dream of writing.

To Kate Strawbridge- for another amazing cover- You brought to life exactly what I wanted- you never fail to amaze me.

And to my readers. Don't stop reading…

FREE STARTER LIBRARY - JOIN MY NEWSLETTER

Get the following titles FREE when you subscribe to my newsletter.

Tee's Newsletter

http://smarturl.it/TeesMailingList

ABOUT THE AUTHOR

I have been a writer from the time I was old enough to recognize that reading was a doorway into my imagination. Poetry was my first foray into the art of the written word. Books were my best friends, my escape, my haven. I am essentially a recluse but this part of my personality is impossible to practice given I have two teenage daughters, who are actually my friends, my tea-makers, my confidantes... I am blessed with a husband who has left me for golf. It's a fair trade as I have left him for writing. We are both passionate supporters of each other's loves – it works wonderfully...

My heart is currently broken in two. One half resides in South Africa where my old roots still remain, and my heart still longs for the endless beaches and the smell of moist soil after a summer downpour. My love for Ma Afrika will never fade. The other half of me has been transplanted to the Land of the Long White Cloud. The land of the Taniwha, beautiful Maraes, and volcanoes. The land of green, pure beauty that truly inspires. And because I am so torn between these two lands – I shall forever remain cross-eyed.

Stalk Tee here:
www.tgayer.com
tee@tgayer.com

 facebook.com/TGAyerAuthor

twitter.com/TGAyerAuthor

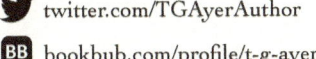 bookbub.com/profile/t-g-ayer